EDUCATING RITA

The door burst open. A young woman he'd never seen before charged into the room, hurtling helplessly towards him. Frank stared at her in some confusion. She looked and sounded like a superior barmaid – and God knew he had enough experience to recognise the type. What was she doing in his study?

They glared at each other, their misunderstanding like hostility. With an effort at patience so obvious it was almost insulting, he said, 'What is your name?'

'Me first name?'

'Well, that would at least constitute some sort of start, wouldn't it?'

Narrow-eyed, she gave him a look of suspicion. But secretly she felt the stirrings of an excited glee. At last he'd sounded like a real professor.

EDUCATING RITA

a novel by

Peter Chepstow

based on the screenplay by
Willy Russell

Star

A STAR BOOK

Published by
the Paperback Division of
W H ALLEN & Co. Ltd

A Star Book
Published in 1983
by the Paperback Division of
W. H. Allen & Co. Ltd
A Howard and Wyndham Company
44 Hill Street, London W1X 8LB

Copyright © Peter Chepstow, 1983

Printed and bound in Great Britain by
Cox & Wyman Ltd, Reading

ISBN 0 352 31356 0

He was not what he seemed. He fitted precisely into the scene, the expected figure, right in every detail of appearance. Yet, as so often, appearance told only the least important part of the story.

'Morning, Dr Bryant,' said the students, and 'Hello, sir.' He waved to them, casually friendly, acting out his role. It came as second nature to him; he would perhaps have denied it was a role. He would have said that he was the man the students saw, tall, bearded, in clothes he didn't bother much about – a good tweed jacket beginning to go comfortably out of shape, an open-necked shirt, jeans: Dr Frank Bryant, Senior Lecturer of this university. If forced to honesty, however, he might have agreed that this was less than the whole truth.

He walked firmly, nevertheless, an established man, fifty years old, work behind him, work still to do. On the university lawns, flocks of students gathered and chattered, broke up, like starlings preparing for migration. So they were, too, he thought: birds of passage. Only he seemed

1

permanent, a fixture. He suppressed thoughts that might lead him to a familiar depression, marched into the high-ceilinged entrance hall of the university. Absent-mindedly friendly in manner, nodding to this and that passing student, he hurried up the stairs, straight-backed and swift-moving, his long hair clean but unkempt, his figure still relatively slim – in the crowd, he thought, he might easily pass for one of the students. He knew this to be an untruth; his self-scrutiny was rigorous, sliding often into self-contempt.

Frank Bryant halted outside a chipped and battered door. He rammed his over-filled briefcase under his left arm, heaved at the door handle, at the same time kicking out sharply at the wood. His actions were automatic; he had performed them a thousand times before. Nor did he really see the chaos that seemed to blur the outlines of the room he entered. It was his room, his study, a symbol and a sanctuary – his workplace. A large desk to one side of the room was almost lost in a turmoil of paper; paper surrounded the large armchair, worn, sagging, beaten into comfort, that stood nearby. A second desk, as burdened as the first, stood by the window. On the wall hung a large print of a Renaissance master-work, one of those paintings in which the religious attempted to sanctify the erotic. And everywhere there were books: they swarmed over the desks, they laid siege to the armchair, small patrols of them were scattered here and there over the floor, and hundreds more stood in regimented rows on the shelves that covered two walls.

It was the books that seemed now to take Frank Bryant's attention. Flinging his briefcase on his desk, he crossed to the shelves. His fingertips ran across the titles, the accumulated art and wisdom of an entire society. They moved past Chaucer, hardly touched Shakespeare's several spines, and left Milton behind. Moderns appeared – Joyce, a clutch of D. H. Lawrences, a Faulkner or two, then E. M. Forster's *Howard's End*. But the fingers stopped at an unexpected choice, Charles Jackson's bestseller, *Lost Weekend*. Slowly, Frank pulled the book from its place. For a moment he glanced at it; then he reached into the gap where it had stood. From the dark recesses at the back of the shelf, he brought out a whisky bottle.

Sitting at his desk, he gulped down his first drink, then sipped his second. He stared out at the sunlight. From a nearby clock-tower, a bell sang out melodiously. Somewhere, a group of students laughed together, the sound bright and silver, thinned by distance. How many times had he sat here, he wondered, and asked himself, as he was asking now, what the hell he was doing? Somehow, at some time, the mainspring of his life had begun to run down; only inertia, he often felt, now kept him going at all. He remembered earlier periods when matters had been very different: periods of enthusiasm, ambition, effort. But they seemed now like episodes in someone else's history. He sighed, and poured himself more whisky. Soon he'd have to go; students were waiting, there was a tutorial to run, knowledge to dispense. With a grimace, he drank, feeling warmth creep through him like resolution, like youth.

It was Blake who was the subject under discussion in the tutorial room. Staring blearily out at the students who faced him, Frank thought, 'Blake, William Blake, the poet Blake . . .' What would Blake have made of this discussion? William and his wife, nude together in their garden, worshipping God and the flesh, earth and spirit. Frank stared out into the sunlight beyond the window, the opinions of his students no more than a faint buzzing in his ears. Blake, he knew, would have laughed the whole enterprise to scorn – the tutorial, the university, Frank Bryant and all.

As if from a distance, he heard an earnest voice declare, 'But in this case, Dr Bryant, is it wise to pursue the metaphysical nature of Blake's poetry?' It was not a voice that seemed to be speaking to him; there was not enough substance in what it said to break into his reverie.

There was silence in the tutorial room. The student who had asked the question, a severe-looking girl called Lesley, waited. The others waited with her, watching Frank. He, as though mesmerised by the sunshine, stared on through the window. Lesley compressed her lips irritably. This was not how she expected her more profound perceptions to be treated. Sharply she called out his name and watched with

3

some pleasure as his head turned towards her, a certain bafflement in its expression. There was a murmur of laughter from the students.

Lesley said, 'I was asking you, Dr Bryant, if you think that in approaching this aspect of Blake we should pursue the metaphysical elements in his poetry?'

'Most definitely!' he said with some heartiness. He watched as Lesley, perplexed, stared down at her books. It bewildered him that they were all getting so worked up about Blake. Blake was certainly not getting worked up about them. 'Blake!' He almost spat the name out. 'Do you know what Blake is? He's a dead poet, that's all.'

'I'm sorry, Dr Bryant, but I can't agree with that.' The student who spoke, a young man named Collins, had always seemed to Frank rather disagreeably humourless. Collins went on, 'To dismiss William Blake as just a dead poet is facile. I've studied Blake extremely closely over a number of years and I must say I disagree absolutely with your own appraisal of his genius . . . Dr Bryant, I don't think you're listening to me!'

Frank, his chair tilted well back, had resumed his examination of the space beyond the window. Now he turned. 'Mr Collins,' he said, 'I don't think you're saying anything to me!' At that moment, his chair began to slip. Wildly he grabbed for the edge of the desk.

Collins asked savagely, 'Doctor, are you drunk?'

'Drunk? Of course I'm drunk! Do you really expect me to teach this . . . this . . . when I'm sober?'

Collins, pale with anger, stood up. 'Then you won't mind if I leave your tutorial.' He marched to the door, his footsteps loud in the silence.

'Mind?' Frank's voice had a note almost of desperation in it. 'Why should I mind? What do you want to be stuck in here for, anyway?'

From the door, Collins said, 'To study literature!'

'Literature!' With a wide gesture Frank took in the sunshine, the clouds, the entire waiting summer world outside the window. 'Look out there! The sun's shining, you're all young – what are you doing in here? Why don't you go out

4

and . . . and do something? Make love. Go out and make love . . . or something . . .'

Collins stared down the room at him, his face white and his eyes malevolent. Then he turned, marched out, slammed the door behind him. There was a strange tense silence in the tutorial room. Frank, behind the desk on the dais, glanced without interest at the waiting students. Then he turned his head away, stared once more out of the window: pale blue sky, soft clouds scattered like freckles, the dark intrusion of a tree. Vaguely he waved his arm at the students, and a moment later heard the scrape and clatter of their movements as they left.

After a while, he sighed. 'We'll carry on with this next time,' he muttered to the empty room.

Plodding across the campus, he heard someone call his name. He turned, puzzled. 'Julia? What are you? . . .'

'Darling, can I have the keys of the car?' She looked at him, frowning slightly, her mouth turned petulantly downward. Her heart-shaped face, he noticed once again, tapered down to a remarkably determined chin. Still, he had to admire her, as she stood there, elegant even in her irritation, her hand out, demanding the keys. Impelled by her gesture, he handed them over.

'I didn't realise your class had finished.'

'Hours ago,' she said, dismissively. 'Frank, remember it's Brian and Elainé for supper tonight.'

Frank, who had turned to go, swung back. 'You do know I'll be late?' Made defensive by the look of dismay on her face, he added, 'I told you. I've got this new student coming.'

'When?'

He shrugged. 'Late. Open University, darling. Though why a grown adult should choose to come to this place after having put in a day's labour already is quite beyond me. Why the devil did I take it on?'

She smiled bitterly. 'You took it on because . . .'

'Don't tell me. I took it on to pay for the drink. I know.' This time he swung away decisively, and resumed his walk across the campus.

'Frank,' she called after him, 'if this dinner has to wait an

5

age for you to turn up and ends up being burned, I'll be very, very cross!'

He raised an arm to show that he'd heard and went on walking. He supposed he liked Julia. After his wife had gone, she'd been a centre of warmth and support, a source of affection, and a recipient of all the affection he'd had left to give. Their lives had intertwined – shared interests, shared sex, shared meals and evenings and nights, parties, quarrels, delights. A life together: Frank and Julia.

Her voice floated after him again. 'And Frank – you won't go to the pub afterwards, will you?' This time he gave no sign that he had heard.

*   *   *   *

She hadn't run away – not quite, not yet. But even standing there was costing her an effort; you could see it in the tension that held her body rigid. Standing in the gateway, she looked small, vulnerable and out of place. White blouse, tight red-and-black striped skirt, black tights, white shoes – her clothes were wrong, neither high-style upper-middle nor sloppy-comfortable academic. Her hair was too elaborately dressed, and its bleached yellow was tinged with pink. She was too young to be a student's mother, too dressed-up to be a canteen worker. What was she doing here, standing stock-still at the university gate?

The long rays of the evening sun behind her made her seem faceless, a silhouette that might vanish at any second. From the shelter of the shadowed gatehouse she stared at what confronted her: bright lawns, grey buildings bound in granite and solemnity, students in slow, chattering groups. She took a deep breath, swallowed, then with a conscious effort stepped forward, walked out into the light. Her features became visible – a small, rather feline face, high cheekboned, with a round chin and long, catlike eyes that, glancing too swiftly from side to side, seemed at this moment to glitter with suspicion.

She would have liked to ask directions from some of the students whom she passed, but didn't dare. Her contempt at

6

her own cowardice couldn't alter the fact that, even when she was able to get her lips apart, no word would pass through them. In the end it was a porter ('Someone my own class,' she thought ruefully) who pointed her up the stairs towards the landing she wanted.

As she climbed, students passed her, calling to each other in confident voices. They gesticulated, flung jokes to and fro, laughed loudly. They carried books. In their loose jerseys, their tee-shirts and denims, they seemed to her unexpectedly classless and conformist, like kids you could see on any street. She'd been expecting posh accents and a sort of BBC-announcer poise.

She tried to listen to what they were saying. At first, nothing seemed to make sense; it was like the radio when the needle sweeps past foreign stations. Then a little group hurried by. One, fair-haired, was shouting over his shoulder at his companions. 'No, no, listen – he actually had to ask, "What's assonance?" Assonance! He didn't have a clue!' Laughing, they ran on down the stairs. For a moment she frowned after them, her lips thoughtfully pursed, then climbed on. She stopped outside a battered door, bending to peer at the name on it: *Dr Bryant*. She swallowed nervously, then knocked. Silence. She knocked again, more firmly. A muffled voice called. Had it asked her to come in? She licked her lips, then turned the handle. The door resisted. She pushed. The door remained firmly closed.

The noise had woken a still-fuddled Frank. He'd fallen asleep in his armchair, empty cup dangling from his fingertips. Now knocking resounded unpleasantly about the room. Hadn't he already called out to whoever was out there? Why the hell didn't they come in? 'Come in!' he yelled.

There seemed to be some sort of scrambling sound outside, a scratching and fumbling. Frank got up, began to shift papers on his desk, not clear yet about what he was doing, what he might be looking for. The knocking began again; it felt like an extension of the headache that was beginning to hammer at his skull. Furiously, he shouted, 'Come in!' and then, as the fumbling sounds restarted,

7

bawled out even more loudly, 'For God's sake, come in!'

The door burst open. A young woman he'd never seen before charged into the room, hurtling helplessly towards him. As she approached, she was already talking, reproach and irritation in her voice. 'I'm comin' in, aren't I? It's that stupid bleedin' handle on the door.' With the aid of furniture, she came to a halt. 'You want to get it fixed!'

Frank stared at her in some confusion. She looked and sounded like a superior barmaid – and God knew he had enough experience to recognise the type. What was she doing in his study? He nodded towards the door. 'Yes,' he muttered. 'Er . . . I suppose you're . . . I've been meaning to . . .'

'Well, that's no good, is it?' Her raucous Liverpudlian cut across his academic genteel. 'Always meaning to? You want to get on with it, because one of these days you'll be shoutin' "Come in" and it'll go on for ever, because the poor sod on the other side won't be able to get in and you won't be able to get out.'

They faced each other, almost glaring, he still bewildered, she in the ferocity that had replaced her earlier nervousness. Feebly, he began again to rummage among the papers on his desk. 'Now,' he said, 'you are . . .'

'I'm what?' she demanded, stiffening with outrage.

Frank's bewilderment increased. 'I beg your pardon?'

'What?'

Once again they glared at each other, their misunderstanding like hostility. His hands moved erratically across the crowded desk. With an effort at patience so obvious it was almost insulting, he said, 'What is your name?'

Understanding at last, she gave a brisk nod. 'Me first name?'

'Well, that would at least constitute some sort of start, wouldn't it?'

Narrow-eyed, she gave him a look of suspicion. But secretly she felt the stirrings of an excited glee. At last he'd sounded like a real professor: *this* was what she'd expected to hear, not a lot of bloody rubbish about a sticking door. She said, 'Rita.'

8

Frank smiled. 'Good.' He might have been congratulating a backward student on answering an easy question. He fumbled again among the papers and found her admission form. His smile faded. 'Rita? . . . Here it says, "Mrs S. White".'

'Ah.' She nodded, but dismissively. 'That's "S" for Susan. That's just me real name. But I'm not a Susan any more. I've changed me name to Rita.' It seemed to her a fact that needed no more explanation: a person surely had the right to pick the name that suited them best. She was irked by this Dr Bryant's continued stare of non-comprehension. She added, hoping to make matters clearer, 'You know – after Rita Mae Brown.'

Frank's bewilderment deepened. Who was this Ms Brown and why had Susan White usurped her name? Was she some benefactress, a member of the family, a rich aunt? He didn't think Mrs White would have any rich aunts.

Rita watched him with growing irritation. She'd come here hoping to find an awe-inspiring intelligence and she'd stumbled on an idiot. 'Rita Mae Brown,' she repeated. 'She wrote *Rubyfruit Jungle*. Haven't you read it? It's a fantastic book.' Dr Bryant continued to gape at her and, with an exasperated gesture, she reached into her bag. 'Here, you wanna lend it?' She hauled out a slightly dog-eared paperback and jabbed it at him. Helplessly, Frank took the book. As he frowned down at it, she asked him, 'And what's your name, then?'

'Frank,' he said. Belatedly, half raising the book, he added, 'Thank you.'

'Frank,' she repeated. 'After Frank Harris?' But he only stared at her: could she have meant Frank Harris, he wondered – *the* Frank Harris?

His scrutiny made her uncomfortable, uneasy. Wasn't Frank Harris one of those names people like him bandied about? She turned from him, and glanced round the room. She said, 'That's a nice picture, isn't it?'

'Yes . . . Yes, I suppose it is . . . er . . . nice . . .'

'It's very erotic.' She peered at him to see what effect the word had had. He was staring at the picture with a puzzled air.

9

He said, 'Actually, I don't think I've looked at it for about ten years – but, yes, I suppose it is erotic.'

'There's no suppose about it. Look at those tits!' Again she peered at him. 'D'you mind me usin' words like that?'

Frank's frown of bewilderment was threatening to become a permanent feature. 'Words like what?' he asked.

'Tits.'

'Oh! No . . .'

Rita felt a lightening of the heart. Perhaps she'd come to the right place after all. 'No,' she said, 'You wouldn't. It's only the masses who don't understand. It's not their fault. But sometimes I hate them. I do it to shock them some-times – you know, at the hairdresser's where I work. I'll say somethin' like, "I'm really fucked!" – dead loud. It doesn't half cause a fuss! But with educated people – they don't worry, do they? It's the aristocracy that swears more than anyone. It's all "Pass the fuckin' pheasant" with them, isn't it? But you can't tell 'em that round our way.'

Frank was beginning to feel like a man in a typhoon. For her part, Rita had swung from terror to relaxation, with a consequent release of energy that came close to euphoria. This Dr Frank Bryant was only a man after all, a human being, head, body, arms, legs – the kind of creature she'd been dealing with all her life. Even here, she thought, even in the university, she could cope, she could have her say. 'Aren't you supposed to be interviewing me?' she asked.

Frank smiled wryly. 'Do I need to?'

She shrugged. 'I talk too much, don't I? I know I talk a lot. I don't at home. But I don't often get a chance to talk to someone like you.' She had a momentary inward glimpse of narrow streets, flowered wallpaper, shirt-sleeved Denny in front of the television, behind the *Sun*. Silence. Clichés. Grunts. Pub sing-songs, creaking bedsprings, fish fingers, washing up . . . 'Can I smoke?' she asked.

'Tobacco?'

It was her turn to be bewildered. 'What? Yeah . . . Oh! Was that a joke?' He smiled. Perhaps the interview was beginning to settle into some manageable pattern. Even if it did, he thought, he had no idea of what its outcome would be. Was this Rita fit to be a student? And if so, did he want her as *his* student? He found himself staring at an out-stretched pack of cigarettes, heard her asking, 'Want one?'

He licked his lips, said dubiously, 'Well, I would love one, but . . .'

'Then have one!'

'I . . . made a promise not to smoke.'

'Well, I won't tell anyone.'

'Promise?' She put the cigarettes on his desk, laid her lighter beside them. As though hypnotised, he took one and lit it.

Rita said, 'I hate smokin' on me own. And everyone seems to have packed up these days. They're all afraid of gettin' cancer. Bloody cowards!'

Hastily, Frank changed the subject. Ash clung to his lapel like a cluster of diseased cells. 'Tell me,' he said, 'what's suddenly led you to this?' He gestured through the window at the green-and-granite of the university courts.

'It's not sudden.' Rita frowned, trying to put words around what had become so clear and certain to her. 'It's not sudden – I've been realising for ages that I was – you know – slightly out of step. See, I'm twenty-six . . .' She paused as though he'd understand the significance of this, then continued when she saw he didn't. 'I should've had a baby by now. Everyone expects it.' In her head she heard querulous questions, saw enquiring or irritated faces: father, mother, husband . . . She wandered to the book-shelves, took down a book. 'But I don't want a baby yet,' she said. Put so baldly, it seemed selfish. 'See, I want to dis-cover meself first. Can you understand that?'

'Yes,' Frank said.

'They wouldn't round our way. They'd think I was mental. I've tried to explain to me husband . . . but between you and me I think he's thick.' Once again she saw Denny's face, his easy smile, his small boy's pout. She cried out as if in desperation, 'He's blind! He doesn't *want* to see!'

Frank, taken aback by her sudden passion, felt once more out of his depth. Rita puffed at her cigarette, blew out smoke. Holding out the book she'd taken from the shelves,

11

she asked, 'What's this like?'

Frank watched it for a moment as though it was about to do him harm. He read out the title. '*Howard's End*?'

Rita giggled. 'Sounds filthy, doesn't it?' She glanced at the author's name. 'E. M. Foster.'

'Forster.' Perhaps, Frank thought, the moment would become significant – the first in which he'd taught her something. He doubted it.

Rita brushed the correction aside. 'What's it like?'

'Read it.' He hesitated, then added, 'Would you like to borrow it?'

'Yeah. All right . . .' She looked down at the book. 'I'll look after it. If I pack the course in, I'll post it back to you.'

'Pack it in? You haven't even started yet!' Why was he encouraging this girl? Did he want her rampaging about his study like this? 'Why should you pack it in?'

She shrugged. 'I just might. I might decide it was a soft idea.' She glanced out of the window, carefully indifferent. 'What does assonance mean?'

Taken off guard, Frank began to laugh. Furiously, she rounded on him. 'Don't laugh at me!' Her strange catlike eyes blazed. He doused laughter, almost afraid. You didn't often see vehemence like that in university studies.

'Well,' he murmured, 'yes – assonance. It's a form of rhyme. What might be a good example? . . . Do you know Yeats?'

'The wine lodge?'

'The poet.'

She shook her head. A dangerous abyss threatened to separate the cultures. Quickly he went on, 'Well, there's a Yeats' poem called *The Wild Swans at Coole*, and in it he rhymes the word "swan" with the word "stone". You see? An example of assonance.'

'Oh.' Was that all there was to it, she thought; no more point than this to all that joking on the stairs? 'It just means gettin' the rhyme wrong?'

It hit Frank quite suddenly that this girl who had come thundering into his room was someone special. She had a mind – idiosyncratic, untutored, stuffed with rubbish, but totally her own. A real mind. Thinking of what she'd said, he began to laugh. 'Well, I've . . . I've never actually looked at it like that, but, yes . . . yes, you could say assonance means getting the rhyme wrong . . . But on purpose, in order to achieve a certain effect.'

She watched him closely, ready to go on the attack if she were being ridiculed. But even she could see that Frank's laughter was genuine and without malice. 'Do you get many students like me?' she asked.

None, he thought. And one was more than enough. She seemed to have filled his study, to be bursting out of its walls. Something about her brightness, about the swiftness of her curiosity, something about her energy and self-confidence seemed to him so much larger than life that he didn't see how he could cope with it. But he said nothing of this, instead pointing out tamely enough that he'd never worked for the Open University before.

'I was dead surprised when they took me,' Rita said. Slanting sunlight made dramatic patterns on the granite facades beyond the window. 'I don't suppose they would've done if it had been a proper university.' He muttered something about the Open University's being designed to embrace a wider intake, but she cut him off. 'You mean they let idiots in?' She watched him try and stammer his way out of that for a little while, then turned away as though he wasn't speaking at all and said, 'I love this room.' Left flat-footed by her change of direction, he could only stare at her. She made a gesture: 'I love the way the light comes in from that window. Do you like it?'

'The window?' He looked at it blankly – was this a genuine sensibility, or was she showing off? If he'd asked Rita, he'd have found her as puzzled as he was. 'I don't often consider that window, as a matter of fact. I sometimes get an urge to throw something through it.'

'What?'

'A student, usually.' For the first time it was she who'd had the wind taken out of her sails. Laughing, she watched him closely. 'You're bleedin' mad, aren't you?'

'Probably.'

13

She swung away, wandered about the room, conscious that from the desk he was scrutinising her like an assayer. She turned to him, a hint of her old ferocity in her stance. 'What you lookin' at?'

'Are you a *good* ladies' hairdresser?'

'Yeah. I am.' She stood with her chin up, as though defying him to doubt her. But then she sagged, shrugged, gave a sigh. 'But they expect too much. Women who come to the hairdressers', they come in and half an hour later they wanna go out a different person. But if you wanna change, you . . . you have to do it from the inside, don't you? You know – like I'm doin'.'

Inside her assertion there was an appeal. Frank saw it, but ignored it. 'Yes,' he said, and walked over to the bookshelves. From its literary recess, he pulled out a bottle. 'Drink?'

'What of?' she asked.

Take whatever you can get, he thought; you'll need your screen against reality, just like the rest of us. But perhaps hers was her dream of a university education. 'Scotch,' he said and, at her nod, poured out two generous slugs.

Rita, without being able to define it, felt this pouring out of drinks to be a ritual of acceptance. Picking up the glass, she looked over its rim at Frank with a new seriousness. It was as if the armour in which she'd entered his room had served its purpose. She could lay it aside – though she'd keep it somewhere handy in case she needed it again. In a different, much quieter voice, she asked, 'D'you think I'll be able to learn?'

Restored to his role of pedagogue, Frank managed a certain measure of pomposity. 'Are you sure you're serious about wanting to learn?'

'I'm dead serious! Look, I know I take the piss and that, but that's only because I'm not . . . you know . . . Confident. But I want to be. Honest.'

He nodded, sipping his drink. Honest was the word. That's the quality Rita had – honesty. He said nothing.

She asked, 'When do you actually . . . you know . . . start teachin' me?'

14

Frank smiled. He felt the whisky stiffening his sinews, summoning up the blood. He said, 'What can I teach you?'

Rita looked distraught, then bewildered. 'Everything,' she answered, simply.

'You want a lot – and I can't give it. Because, between you, me and the walls, I'm actually an appalling teacher. Most of the time it doesn't matter – appalling teaching is quite in order for most of my appalling students. But not for you, young woman.' He began to shove books and papers into the frayed leather of his briefcase, ignoring her wide-eyed dismay. 'All I know – and you must listen to this . . . All I know is that I know absolutely nothing.' His self-knowledge seemed to him at the same time too acute and too banal. He retreated into a jocularity which, perhaps, told another truth. 'Besides, I've decided I don't like the hours for this Open University business. They expect us to teach when the pubs are open.' He walked to the door; turning, he saw her stricken face. 'I'm sorry,' he said. He opened the door with a formality he recognised as false, theatrical. 'There are other tutors. I'll arrange it for you . . . post it on.'

For a moment they faced each other. Both felt rejected, she brutally, he as though by himself. It was as if he'd offered himself a chance, then turned it down. Rita suddenly pushed out her chin, switched her gaze past him, marched without a word out of the room. 'Goodbye,' he'd said, but she hadn't waited for that.

The room seemed strangely silent, musty. It smelled of old dust and disintegrating paper. He was suddenly conscious that almost all the books on his shelves had been written by men and women now dead. He'd told his students to abandon Blake and rush out into the sunlight. Now he felt as though he'd deliberately turned away from an open door, the chance of fresh air, the possibility of new discoveries. He slapped his briefcase shut, poured the last of the whisky in his cup down his throat and walked from the room.

She was waiting for him behind a granite buttress, lurking in ambush like a guerilla in the educational jungle. Her voice was harder, more strident; she came, he thought, from a tradition of practiced harridans.

'Listen to me!' she said. Her heels clacked as they walked as though machine-guns backed her arguments. 'You're my tutor and you're gonna bleedin' well teach me!'

He tried to repeat what he'd told her upstairs, that there were other teachers, but she cut him short. '*You're* my tutor! I don't want another tutor!'

Exasperated, he turned to face her. They glared at each other like people about to fight. 'For God's sake, woman, I've told you . . .'

'You're my tutor!' She was waving a form in his face. 'You're my tutor! Look! It says here . . .'

'I've told you,' he shouted. 'I've told you I don't want to do it. Why come to me?'

'Because you're a crazy, mad piss-artist who wants to throw his students through the window.' She looked up at him, driven into further honesty. 'And I like you. Don't you recognise a compliment?'

He felt complimented. More, he felt refreshed, invigorated. He said, 'Do you think I could have another cigarette?'

'You can have these.' Rita smiled, handed him the pack. 'And I'll bring my scissors next week and give you a haircut.'

Lighting a cigarette, he mumbled, 'You're not coming here next week.'

'I am. And you're gettin' your hair cut. I suppose you want to walk about like that, do you?'

'Like what?'

'Like a geriatric hippie!' With a beam of malicious joy she turned away, marched off up the path. Bemused, he watched her determined strut, her small, square shoulders, her firm rump. Suddenly she stopped, turned round, began to bear down on him again. He braced himself for another broadside. She said, 'Goin' the wrong way, wasn't I?' and swept past him.

Watching her receding figure, he found himself fingering the hair at the back of his neck. Is that how he seemed to her –

a geriatric hippie? How many other people would take a similar view, he wondered. He rather thought that he himself would be amongst them.

Rita, homeward bound on the top of a bus, felt utterly elated. She had marched into the Promised Land and staked her claim to a piece of it, marched right in, overcome her awe, conquered her fear and taken possession of something she already thought of as hers by right. She smiled to herself, thinking of Frank Bryant, his bewilderment, the whisky hidden behind his books, his final feeble attempt to palm her off on someone else. She'd shown *him*! She glanced sideways at the young man beside her: dark hair, glasses, neat jacket, large book at which he peered with ostentatious concentration.

Rita smiled again. From her bag she took out *Howard's End* and began to read. But very soon the words seemed to empty of meaning. There were too many of them on the page and what they had to tell her seemed slow and dry. She became aware of the young man watching her and, slapping shut the book, confronted him. 'Are you familiar with Forster?'

How could she know that it was Collins she'd asked, with his regulation opinions kept polished by constant application of the regulation critics? Brusquely she cut short his rhapsodies. 'Between you and me, I think he's crap!' Delighted by his consternation, she leaned closer. 'You're a student, aren't you?'

Collins nodded curtly, then, as though recalled to his duties, opened his book again.

Rita made a smug face. She half-closed her eyes, like a purring cat. In a crisp, carrying voice she said, 'So am I!'

*   *   *   *

The house was unexpectedly grand. It stood in a Georgian terrace, dignified in its proportions and protected by iron railings. Frank was always quick to point out that when he'd bought it, the area had been run down and the house seedy. Sometimes he would add that nothing had really changed

17

because as the house had grown more splendid, its owner had become seedier: 'the sum of dilapidation has remained constant.'

Frank was not in the house now. Indeed, there were few signs of his presence. The easy but disordered comfort that marked his study was entirely missing here. Julia had made it her kingdom. With her long, dark hair, her firm teacher's voice and her black eyes, part shoe-buttons, part lasers, she had taken over the shape and structure, as well as the running, of their joint household. Whatever had sagged or wobbled had been thrown out. Stripped pine furniture, suitable prints, amusing knick-knacks, functional lamps – the interiors told a familiar contemporary story.

In the dining room, Julia was putting the finishing touches to her table settings. She pushed a glass this way, then that, rearranged flowers, straightened a knife. Her movements were oddly nervous for so deliberately gracious a room. She was frowning, either in concentration or in anger. Through an open door came the sounds of a Mozart piano concerto.

Julia sighed, then walked through the door into the sitting room beyond. Her guests smiled as she came in, Brian Thomas standing in the middle of the room, his wife Elaine sitting back in an armchair, enraptured by the music. Her long hair curled about pale features, and her eyes were closed. She, like her husband, held a glass of pale sherry.

Brian was a neatly built, compact man. His wide, rather thin-lipped mouth should have been that of a humorous man, but his anxious eyes and over-neat hair belied that. The lines on his face and his firm, cleft chin gave him the appearance of strength, but this too was contradicted by the eyes, and the weak mobility of the mouth. Brian Thomas was compounded of such contradictions, with the result that people's opinion of him varied wildly. While some would trust him with their last pound note, others were careful never to turn their backs on him. Younger than Frank, and arriving at the university where they both taught several years later, Brian had nevertheless achieved an authority there which had always eluded, or never been sought, by Frank. Brian's complex – some said devious – nature had

18

made him into an instinctive politician: he swam through the intrigues of university life with the ease of a goldfish in a pond.

He poured more sherry – 'Well, as Frank's not here yet . . .' – and, with their refilled glasses, all three remained silent for a moment. From the depths of her chair, Elaine murmured, 'Lovely record, Julia,' and Julia smiled a harassed agreement.

'I hope he won't be long,' she said. Elaine smiled, Brian frowned through the window. Again they remained without speaking. Abruptly, Brian put down his glass.

'God, I forgot – I meant to phone my publisher! May I, Julia?'

She smiled agreement, drifting back into the dining room. Brian came hurrying after her, swinging the door shut behind him. The telephone stood on a corner table. He glanced at it for a moment, then swung away from it. Julia faced him, her face pale now, and her expression nervous. Without a word Brian took her in his arms and kissed her with a desperate passion.

'Brian . . .' Julia's whisper was part acceptance, part warning.

'Darling,' said Brian. 'Darling.'

They were deep in the intertwinings of another kiss when the front door slammed with a cheerful crash. They leapt apart.

'Frank!' Julia gasped. Distraught, they stared at each other. Then Brian was hurtling across the room to the telephone. Receiver pressed to ear, he was soon deep in the contrivances of his fictitious conversation – 'Yes, I know that, Morgan . . . I know that, but it's not as though this were the first book of mine you'd ever done . . .'

In the sitting room, Julia, just a touch breathlessly, was saying to Frank, 'You didn't go to the pub?' It sounded as though, even with the evidence of her eyes, she didn't really believe this.

'Changed my mind,' said Frank. He wandered towards the dining room, stood in the doorway, listening to the embattled Brian.

19

Raising his voice, Brian said into the dead mouthpiece, 'Morgan, it's imperative that the book is published before the next academic year commences.' As he spoke, he raised a hand in Frank's direction, the careless greeting of an old friend. 'All right, Morgan . . . all right. I'll phone again tomorrow . . . Goodbye.' He put the phone down, smiled, shrugged in apology. 'Sorry about that, Frank – my publisher . . .'

Frank strolled past him and Brian, with a quick movement, closed the door of the room. With what seemed a conscious effort, he adjusted the expression on his face, taking on the appearance of one sorrowfully magisterial, the mask of a headmaster about to admonish a favourite pupil.

'Frank,' he said. 'Ah . . . I wanted . . . ah . . . to mention this before we dined. Slightly embarrassing, but . . .'

Frank was looking at him with eyebrows raised and a slight smile on his lips. He looked like a disenchanted uncle watching the antics of a precocious child.

'Thing is,' Brian went on, 'the thing . . . ah . . . is – there's been a bit of a complaint.'

'Complaint?'

'Apparently you were a little . . . ah . . . drunk. At your tutorial today.'

'No,' Frank said firmly.

'No?'

'No. I was a lot drunk.'

The two men faced each other, their roles now reversed. Frank looked like a happily delinquent child, Brian like his harassed parent. Brian groaned. 'Frank! . . . Oh, Frank, why do you do it? When you've got . . .' He waved his hand at the middle-class splendour that surrounded them. Had the gesture included Julia? 'Well, what *haven't* you got?' he asked, almost querulously.

Frank smiled down at him. Sometimes he felt that his height was the only advantage over Brian that he had. Even that hadn't been of his own making. 'What I haven't got at the moment,' he said, 'is a drink.'

Brian sighed, still in his parental role. 'Frank, the staff

accept that you . . . I mean, we all understand that you drink. But I don't think . . . I really don't think that the signs should be displayed to the students.'

'Brian, do you know what assonance is?' Frank asked.

Brian stared at him. 'Of course.'

'Go on.'

'Assonance?' He watched Frank's face narrowly. Was it a trick question? Was some tell-tale midden of ignorance about to be exposed? Frank nodded encouragement and Brian said, cautiously, 'Assonance is a rhyme, the identity of which depends only upon the vowel sounds. An assonance is a merely syllabic resemblance.'

To his annoyance, Frank was laughing, an almost silent laugh that indicated some private joke.

'Assonance,' said Frank, 'means getting the rhyme wrong!'

*　　　*　　　*　　　*

It was as if time had settled the matter. When Rita came a second time to see Frank, it seemed to have been tacitly accepted by both of them that he would be her tutor, she his student. On this second visit, she was oddly subdued. Perhaps her first assault on education's citadel had been so violently energetic that now she was in the throes of a reaction. Nevertheless, the fact of her, her honesty, and her hunger for a learning of which she hardly understood the nature, haunted Frank. He struggled, not understanding the feeling: it was a long time since he'd had any sense of purpose in his teaching, or in any other department of his life.

In his teens, in his twenties, Frank had burned. The idea of talent had consumed him. Greatness had beckoned; his life had been dedicated to achievement. He'd written, and his poems had been taken seriously by people he'd respected, and therefore, in reflection, by himself. Teaching had seemed to him essentially nothing more than a way to subsidise his poetry. Nevertheless, he'd thought of himself as an inspirer, a natural leader, a man whose own enthusiasms

21

would kindle a responsive fire in his students. Then the years had passed. Poetry had fled. For a long time he'd searched for it, with an increasing desperation; then he'd turned from it in a profound, yet profoundly self-deceiving, disgust. What had been left was his university career, rendered meaningless now, since of itself it had never seemed enough. The generations of students had passed before him, receptacles into which he'd poured the necessary quantities of established opinion. Blake, Wordsworth, Shelley, Keats – work that had meant less and less to him had been more and more mechanically explained to an endless succession of classes to whom poetry meant nothing. 'For them,' he'd said once, 'for our dear students, poetry is a sort of raw material and the university the factory in which they process it into acceptable consumer goods – the standard degrees regarded as so desirable by the employment market.'

Into this long-established cynicism, increasingly moderated by alcohol and self-disgust, his strange new student now obtruded week by week. The fact that, despite his best effort, it was *he* whom she wanted as teacher had had an unsettling effect on him. The fact that it wasn't just a bankable degree that she was after, but that she wanted so desperately to learn, had deepened his bewilderment. Her odd, knowing innocence had made him see the shallow sophistication of the university in a new light. Its standards seemed to him more clearly than ever before to be false ones, its students and teachers both to be whoring after false gods. To his own astonishment, he found himself beginning to drink less.

Still, waiting for her to appear again in his university study, he was about to take a small, protective nip when, his hand already on the bottle, he heard a faint metallic movement at his door. He glanced at it: the handle was moving in an indeterminate manner, waggling first one way, then the other. No one, however, was making any attempt actually to open the door. Staring at this suddenly idiosyncratic handle, Frank moved across to it. He took a deep breath, then yanked the door open.

22

Bent double, Rita crouched in the corridor outside. She looked up at him. There was a moment of silence. Then she extended her hand. The long dispenser of an oilcan pointed at him like the muzzle of a gun.

'Hello,' said Rita. 'I was just oilin' it for you.' Straightening, she walked past him into the room, her expression serene. As she came by, she handed him the oilcan. 'You can have that,' she said, as though giving him something he'd long coveted. He shut the door and watched her, smiling, as she began to prowl to and fro.

'Don't you ever just walk into a room and sit down?' he asked.

'I don't want to sit down. I like walkin' around this room . . . I love that lawn down there. All the proper students . . .' Wistfully, she stared down into the court.

Frank joined her at the window. 'Why didn't you become what you call a "proper student"?'

Rita snorted. 'What? After goin' to the school *I* went to?'

'Bad?'

'No. Just normal.' She shrugged. 'Boring – you know. Ripped-up books, broken glass everywhere, knives, fights . . . And that was just the staff room!'

They laughed, but both recognised the humour as defensive. The reality she remembered was banal enough – the usual inner-city school, an uneasy cross between a youth club and a Borstal.

'No,' she said, 'they tried their best, I suppose. Always tellin' us we stood more of a chance if we studied . . . But you don't listen, do you? 'Cos if you did that, you'd have to change – and that's not allowed. So, you forget about it. Go out, buy yourself another new dress. Or play another record and tell yourself life's great . . . Till one day – I dunno why – one day you . . . own up to yourself and you say, "Is this it? Is this the absolute maximum I can expect from this livin' lark?" . . .'

Absorbed, Frank was watching her, listening to her – almost trying to *be* her. He wanted to understand, in some way to contain, her experience. She was so completely in the present moment, so utterly the person she presented, with so little pretence, so few and such tattered masks, that she seemed profoundly mysterious to him. He'd grown used to games players, to people consciously acting the parts they thought life – usually, university life – required of them. Her honesty baffled him. Or was it just that the roles she played were unfamiliar to him?

For Rita, the subject was finished. Time was going by: remembering the past, she'd recalled the necessities of the present. 'Come on,' she said. 'Let's start.'

For a moment Frank was confused by her change of direction. But he was beginning to get used to her unpredictability. He searched among the papers on his desk, hauled out her essay.

'Crap?' Rita half-asked, half-asserted.

Frank laughed. 'No, no. Or . . . The thing is . . .' He frowned, serious now, the responsible teacher. 'Rita, how the hell can you write an essay on E. M. Forster with almost total reference to Harold Robbins?'

'You said bring in other authors. "Reference to other works will impress the examiners," you said.'

'I said refer to other works. But I don't think the examiner, God bless him, will have read . . .' – he consulted her essay – '. . . *Fifty-Nine Park Avenue*.'

Rita looked at him, a stubborn expression on her face. 'Well, that's his hard luck, isn't it?'

Frank sighed. How did you teach discrimination without imposing your own tastes? It was in the end precisely what education was about – the establishment of standards, and of methods by which one might arrive at them. But with Rita, at her age, all he could say was 'Forster good, Robbins bad' and nothing would be gained by making an assertion of that kind. He could hear already her jeering, 'Yeah – who says?'

'It'll be your hard luck when he fails your paper,' he said. 'Which he would do if you wrote like this during an exam.'

Rita exploded, her voice as raucous as a jay's. 'Oh, that's prime, isn't it? I get failed, just 'cos I'm more well read than the frigging examiner!'

Driven to it, Frank responded acidly, 'Devouring pulp

fiction is not being well read.'

'I thought readin' was supposed to be good for one!'

'It is,' he agreed. There was no point in arguing. 'Only you have to be selective . . . In your favour, you do mention – let's see – yes, in here: *Sons and Lovers*. But it's . . . it's . . . well, all over the place.' He tapped at the paper, like an executioner testing his axe. Rita watched him, her face set. But this time the look expressed determination, not her previous stubborn anger. 'It's very subjective,' he went on, 'and slightly sentimental.'

'Crap!' said Rita, nodding. She had, she felt, abruptly stumbled on something important. Her work wasn't her. There was no need to defend it as though anything wrong with it would see her condemned as a person without worth. It was when Frank had used the word 'subjective' that she'd suddenly realised this. Work was what one did, not what one was. Maybe it was knowing this that made university people so different from the people she knew: they could disagree without feeling the need to draw blood. Real blood, not the kind of wounds words made. 'Crap!' she said again. 'Right?'

Frank shook his head. 'No. There's a lot in the essay that's . . . well, worthy of . . .' But he couldn't define what was positive in it. He only knew it wouldn't win her any marks in an exam. 'You see, the main thing, Rita, is that if you're going to learn criticism, then you have to begin to discipline that mind of yours.'

But Rita's mind, undisciplined, had already wandered off. 'Are you married?' she asked, abruptly.

'What?'

'Are you? . . . What's your wife like?'

'For God's sake, woman!' Frank was genuinely exasperated. 'Is my wife at all relevant?'

Rita shrugged. 'You should know – you married her!'

Frank hesitated. These were, weren't they, dangerous paths? He said, firmly, 'No, she is *not* relevant. I haven't seen her for a long time. We split up. All right?'

'I'm sorry.'

'Why are you sorry?'

'I'm sorry for askin'. For bein' nosey.'

With a sharp nod, Frank responded to her contrition. He said, 'Listen – the thing about *Howard's End* is that when . . .'

'Why did you split up?' Rita was looking at him wide-eyed. She really wanted to know, just as she did when the customers at her hairdressers' let out their marital secrets. She followed her curiosity in the way that hounds followed a fox. It was her nature. When on that scent she was totally concentrated, absorbed as by a good story.

'Perhaps you'd like to take notes!' Frank said. 'When you have to answer a question on Forster, you can treat the examiner to an essay called *Frank's Marriage!*'

'Oh, go away – I'm only interested.' And she was. Avidly.

Frank got to his feet, strolled to the window. Why the hell had he and his wife split up? Come to that, why had they ever got together? It must have seemed over-whelmingly right at the time. Now, looking back, it made no sense – he could remember the actions, the events, but he'd long forgotten the reasons. He sighed, and said what he thought might well have been true. 'We split up, Rita, because of poetry.'

'You what?' Aghast, she stared at him.

'One day my wife pointed out to me that for fifteen years my output as a poet had dealt exclusively with that period in which we . . . discovered each other.'

'Are you a poet?'

'Was . . . And so, to give me something new to write about, she left. A very noble woman, my wife. She left me for the good of literature. And, remarkably . . . it worked!'

'You wrote a lot of good stuff?'

'I stopped writing altogether.'

Rita sat straighter. 'Are you takin' the piss?'

Frank laughed. 'No,' he said. If he was, the joke was on him.

Rita said, 'People don't split up because of things like that. Because of literature!'

'Maybe you're right. But that's how I remember it.' He'd

turned back to the window again. It wasn't how he remembered it. He remembered squalid rows, despair, deceit – but why? What on earth had all that been about?

'D'you live on your own, then?'

Suddenly irritated by this trivial catechism, he turned round. 'Rita!'

'I was only askin'.'

He hesitated. She was only asking. He said, 'I live with a girl. Her name is Julia. She's very caring, very tolerant . . . admires me enormously.' Another half-truth – he had no idea what Julia thought of him these days.

'And . . . do you like her?'

Did he? Well, of course he did! 'I like her enormously. It's myself I'm not too fond of.'

'Ah – you're great!'

Frank smiled sardonically. One of these days, she'd learn discrimination. He could help her with books; with people, she was on her own. 'A vote of confidence,' he said. 'Thank you. But I'm afraid you'll find there's less to me than meets the eye.'

'See?' Rita was flushed, like a small child at a circus, excited by the lions, an animal act, perhaps the clowns. 'Look, you can say dead clever things like that, can't you? I wish I could talk like that. It's brilliant!'

'Staggering.' Her enthusiasm made him uneasy; it was misplaced and, when directed at him, possibly bogus. It was time to return to Forster. 'Now look – the point about *Howard's* . . .'

'Oh, leave that!' She pleaded like a child. 'I just like talkin' to you. It's great . . . That's what they do wrong in schools, you know. They get you talkin' and that, and you're all havin' a great time talkin' about somethin' – and the next thing they wanna do is turn it into a lesson.'

'Yes. That, Rita, is what we call education.' If he was drawn into her anarchic disregard of the world's rules, he'd be of no further use to her. So he told himself; in fact, he was terrified that, once inside the happy chaos of her anarchy, he'd never find his way out.

'You'd think there was something wrong with education,

to hear you talk.' She'd missed his terror, picked up his disillusion. He saw her suddenly as a waif, someone too long abandoned. Now she was too naïve, too ignorant, too innocent and honest – put simply, just too late. 'Ah, Rita – why didn't you walk in here twenty years ago?' he suddenly exclaimed. And thought to himself, fleetingly, 'In time to save me.'

She laughed. "Cos I don't think they'd have accepted me at the age of six.'

'You know what I mean.'

'I know. But it's not twenty years ago, Frank. It's now. You're there, and I'm here.'

'Yes – and you're here for an education. You must keep on reminding me of that. Come on. Forster!'

She made a grimace. 'Ah – forget him!'

For a moment he looked at her without speaking. Part of him was eagerly agreeing with her: right – forget Forster. For now, for always. But she had need of him. Come to that, he had need of himself. For the moment, anyway. So, no weakening: Bryant's last stand. He pushed his face into the right expression of pedagogic anger. 'Now, you listen to me. You said I was going to teach you. You want to learn. Well, that, I'm afraid, means a lot of work. You've barely had basic schooling; you've never passed an examination in your life. Possessing a hungry mind is not in itself a guarantee of success!'

She wriggled, like a little girl faced with a dish she detested. 'But I just don't like *Howard's* bleedin' *End*!'

'Then go back to what you do like, and stop wasting my time.' The irritation now was genuine. 'You go out and buy yourself a new dress, and I'll go to the pub.'

For just a moment, there was bewilderment in her eyes. She frowned. 'Is that you putting your foot down?'

'It is, actually.'

She nodded, taking this in. For the first time, she had the feeling that she was involved in a real transaction, that this room and the Frank Bryant who sat in it were part of the actual world, the same world she lived in on all the other days of the week. She smiled at him. 'Aren't you impressive when you're angry?'

Frank gave a groan of mock-despair, then both of them were laughing. But when the laughter had died away, she hauled out her books, sighed, opened *Howard's End*, opened a notebook, and waited with a new alertness for the tutorial to begin.

*   *   *   *

The streets shone, made slick by water. For the moment, though, the rain had stopped. Rita side-stepped puddles, leaped off kerbs to avoid choked gutters. These were narrow streets, lined by low, slate-roofed houses. Here and there great towers varied the skyline, pushing up beyond the terrace ridges, featureless, repetitive, like temples to some presiding god of monotony. Elsewhere, all buildings had been torn away: the city gaped, its muddy roots exposed, prepared for a renewal already as defeated, even on the drawing board, as the poverty-stricken areas that had been demolished. The low hillocks of these sad expanses were dotted with an oddly unvarying detritus – ripped-open mattresses, soggy cardboard boxes, burnt-out cars, abandoned prams, a filthy snow of discarded paper.

Rita saw and did not see all this: it was the townscape in which she'd passed her life. Yet, as always, it set up a slow, subliminal turmoil within her, a turmoil that nowadays never subsided. Everything in her world dissatisfied her – yet she had no other. Her work, and perhaps even more her status, as a student seemed to her to be opening up an escape route, but it would be a long time before she'd be ready to make a break. Perhaps she never would be. Perhaps when she tried her escape, she'd somehow be hauled back, retried, condemned to solitary confinement for life. And, in any case, what of the meantime? Suspended between a past she increasingly saw as inadequate, as mean and limiting, she'd not yet attained a future, that spacious future, filled with knowledge, opportunity and good talk after which she hankered, a future in which she would at last be able to move unfettered, owner of the culture to which now she was only a claimant.

She approached her street, as undistinguished as the rest. But familiar, and lined after all with the houses of friends. Women called out to her – 'All right, girl?' She waved, called back. Familiar doorways, dogs that knew her too well to bark, kids with dirty faces running past. The telephone box where she crossed the road. Blue door, blue window frames, a leaning bicycle: home.

The house sounded like the inside of a brass band's big bass drum. She stood in the tiny hall, wide-eyed with horror. Had the demolition gangs missed a street and struck here by mistake? The regular thumps seemed to be shaking every wall in the little building. She opened a door. Bare floor, piled furniture, dust. Through the dust she could see a man, tall, with dark, curly hair, a great hammer in his hand. As she watched, the hammer swung, bit deep into the marshalled flowers of the wallpaper. Dust flew, plaster dropped in a small avalanche, inner brickwork softened and fell away.

'Denny! What the frig are you doin'?'

Her husband swung round to face her. He had heavy dark eyebrows, but a loose, self-indulgent mouth, a tip-tilted, schoolboy's nose, dark eyes that seemed made to search out things to laugh about. He was laughing now, hefting the hammer, sweat gleaming on his forehead. 'What's it look like? I'm takin' this wall down.'

'Why?'

'I got bored.' He turned, swung the hammer again. Brickdust exploded around him. The hole in the wall expanded. Over his shoulder, he said, 'I thought we could make these two rooms into one through lounge. Improve the house.'

Rita stared past him, through the hole, into the other room. Against the far wall, a gaudy cocktail cabinet glowed back at her. Seen against each other, the two wallpapers seemed to her to clash horribly. 'There's only one way you could improve this house,' she stated firmly. 'By bombing it!'

'Ah, go away.' The hammer swung again. 'It'll look

great, this, when I've finished. Once I've got the plaster up, you won't recognise it.'

He began to push dust and rubble aside with his foot. Rita moved closer to him, watching the movements of his back, of his slim buttocks and thighs. She looked down, traced a pattern on the dust that now covered a displaced table. Abruptly she said, 'Denny, come to the theatre with me.'

He faced her, astonishment all over his dirt-streaked face. 'What for?'

'To see a play?'

It still made no sense to him. 'Why?'

'Go on. Just come.'

'Sod off!' As though she'd threatened his very masculinity, he turned back to the wall. Again he hefted the hammer, the action this time over-dramatised. A man doing man's work.

Rita watched him thoughtfully. The hammer crashed into the wall. She was beginning to feel irritated: she'd made an effort to bridge the canyon between her two worlds and she deserved a better response than this. At the same time, she knew this was not true: there had never been a chance that the canyon could be bridged and, in any case, she deserved nothing. Her irritation grew.

'I've got to do this essay, see?' she said. 'For me tutor. Listen – "Suggest ways in which one might deal with some of the staging difficulties in a production of Ibsen's *Peer Gynt*." Have you got any relevant thoughts on that, Denny?' The hammer crashed into the wall once more. 'Denny, if we went to the theatre, we could see the play and it'd help me to do me essay.' Was she really attempting to persuade him, or building herself an alibi – later she could say that at least she'd tried. Her husband beat wordlessly at the walls of the matrimonial home. 'Denny! . . .'

Over his shoulder he wailed, 'I don't want to know!' Another savage blow of the hammer. Dust billowed about him as he rounded on her. 'I've told you, Susan. I don't like you doin' this. Right? Now just leave me out of it!'

'Why?' she asked, stubbornly. But she knew why.

31

'I've told you. I don't wanna go.'

The hammer blows resounded, the walls trembled, dust and splinters flew. For a moment longer she watched him. Rita confronts Susan, she thought wryly. Perhaps it all belonged in an intelligence test: if Denny is married to Susan, who is Rita's husband? She turned away, already reaching into her bag for the copy of *Peer Gynt*.

'Where you goin'?' Denny called after her.

'I'm goin' upstairs, with *Peer Gynt*.'

'With who?' Dark eyes peered suspiciously at her through the dust clouds. She waved the book at him in wordless explanation. He made a suddenly disappointed face, like that of a small boy denied sweets. 'I thought we were goin' down the Bierkeller tonight.'

'What for?'

'For a laugh,' he said, in an exasperated voice. 'For a drink. It's great down there. You've never been, have you? Do you know they've eight different kinds of beer to choose from?'

Rita mocked astonishment. 'Well! Isn't that remarkable! Who'd have thought that they'd build Paradise at the end of our street!'

Upstairs, she spread herself across the bed, notebook ready to catch her thoughts. No thoughts came. Instead, her brain seemed to shudder in rhythm with the thudding of the hammer downstairs. The walls of the little house vibrated. Scowling ferociously, she tried to concentrate on Ibsen, but all she could think of was that the foundations were under assault – the foundations of the house, of her marriage, of her entire life.

'You know what's wrong with you, don't you, Susan?' Denny's voice came booming up the narrow stairs. Rita slammed shut her book.

'Well,' she shouted back, 'what *is* wrong with me?'

'You need a baby!'

Her face twisted up into an expression of bored disgust. There it was, the universal cure-all, the constant option, the one totally acceptable function. 'Do I?' she called down the stairs.

'How long is it since you stopped takin' the Pill?'

Dear God! The Pill! She leaped from the bed, rolled back a corner of the carpet, lifted a loose floorboard. The oblong card of pills lay half-used in its pack. Quickly she took one out and, as Denny loudly repeated his question from below, swallowed it down.

'December!' she yelled. 'I stopped in December.' She felt guilty. She was deceiving Denny, robbing him of something he valued above everything else. In families like the ones they'd both grown up in, children justified all hardships, all relationships, all misdeeds and weaknesses. She was robbing him of his justification. With a sigh, she walked from the room.

Denny, still shouting, was hammering at a stubborn section of wall. 'I mean, that's nearly five months ago. You're still not pregnant. I think we'd better get you to a doctor.' Swinging back the hammer, he suddenly became aware of her behind him, leaning against the doorpost. He gave her a glance, struck the wall another blow. 'It can't be anything wrong with *me*,' he said, confidently. 'I come from an extremely fertile strain. The fellers in our family only have to look at a woman and she's pregnant.'

Rita giggled. 'Must be 'cos you're all cock-eyed!'

They both laughed now, as much at their own laughter, at the renewed togetherness it signalled, as at her joke. Denny swung the hammer again, but the wall still resisted.

'Come on,' said Rita/Susan. 'Get ready. I thought we were goin' to the Bierkeller.'

'I thought you were doin' your studyin'.'

'How can I do me bleedin' essay with you demolishin' the house around me ears?' She laughed. She felt unexpectedly as though after all there might be a chance that she'd be happy. She felt Rita melting, Susan taking over. Was that the formula for happiness – the price?

Denny said, 'All right – I'll just finish this, then I'll get changed.' He swung the hammer, drove it at the wall. The house shook.

'Go on!' yelled Rita – yelled Susan. 'Go on – hit it!' She laughed. 'Hit it!'

He laughed with her. 'You can't just belt it, you know. It has to be taken down carefully.'

But she was beyond such expertise. 'Go away! Hit it! Go on!'

'Gah – what do you know about it?' He began looking about him. 'Now, where's the small hammer gone?' He scuffed at the rubble around his feet, then sighed and walked out to the kitchen. She could hear him in there, rummaging about.

She stared at the wall. She saw again his muscular arms, rising, then driving down. The movement, the force of it, seemed almost sexual: she thought of his narrow buttocks thrusting between her thighs. The image excited her, yet at the same time made her angry. Bloody men, keeping women in their place with sex, with muscle-power, with noise. Bloody men, bullying their way to an authority they never earned.

On an impulse, she stepped forward. She picked up the hammer he'd left leaning against the wall. Its weight seemed to challenge her; she hefted it as he had done, feeling her body tense as if for effort. She took a deep breath, shut her eyes, and flung the hammer-head at the wall with all her strength. She heard Denny hurrying back, but was past caring now. She hit the wall again, thrusting her hips and shoulders into the blow. There was an explosive crash that seemed for a second to envelop her. The entire top segment of the wall began to slide towards the floor. Bricks tumbled past her, mortar flew in a rain of chips. As the collapsed section hit the ground, a great cloud of dust rose up, as though the room had been hit by a shell. She stepped back in triumph, then turned to grin at Denny.

He was peering up at the ceiling with an expression of horrified surprise on his face. She followed his gaze. Part of the ceiling had fallen. One of the main beams supporting the upper floor had been exposed. One end, now left with nothing holding it, was sagging at an ominous angle. They looked at each other in alarm. Seeing her in her clown's make-up of dismay and plaster dust, he began to laugh.

'You're a mad bitch, you are!' he exclaimed. 'You're still my girl, aren't you?'

She wriggled her hips, put on a sexy pout. 'I could be . . . if you play your cards right.'

They looked into each other's eyes, waiting for the flesh to offer them its customary deceits. Then, laughing again, they moved closer. He put his arms around her, she raised her dust-covered face for his kiss. She could feel the heat of his loins against hers. Was she Rita? Was she Susan? She opened her lips to his tongue, thrust herself against him. Bugger the questions, she thought to herself: let them wait.

*　　　*　　　*　　　*

Frank Bryant, walking with colleagues along the university corridors, spoke of departmental politics. There was talk of promotion, tenure, a Chair soon to be vacant. Though contributing to the conversation, he gave it only a part of his attention. The rest of his mind, as so often recently, was busily contemplating that continuing phenomenon, his Open University student. He no longer struggled against his obsession with Rita; rather, he debated with himself increasingly what the exact nature of that obsession was. Admiring her qualities, he remained conscious of her vulnerability. Yet in herself she was a force that had somehow begun to alter his life – his perception of himself, his sense of purpose. But that wasn't, was it, why he was obsessed with her? Surely it was his obsession which had made such powerful effects possible? . . . Thus he argued the matter round and round in his head, while still gravely discussing whether a man named Grantley or another named Wilshaw would be more suitable as Reader in Anglo-Saxon Studies. In passing, someone mentioned Brian Thomas. 'Ah, yes – Brian . . .' Frank said, sighing.

At that very moment Brian was leaning tensely across Julia's desk. Julia, nervous, was sitting well back in her chair.

'Look,' she said, 'we agreed. If you're seen in my room, it would . . .'

35

Urgently, Brian interrupted her. 'I'm going to leave Elaine.' He watched Julia as, white-faced with the shock, she stood up and walked to the window. He followed her. 'You must leave Frank,' he said, firmly. He reached for her as she shook her head fiercely, murmuring something about how much Frank still needed her. 'Needs you!' he echoed. 'My God – most of the time he can't even *see* you!'

'That's not true. He *does* need me – he responds to me.'

'Is that why he's always four-parts pissed?' Brian clearly felt it was time to put the boot in.

'Recently he's hardly been drinking. It's taken me a long time, but at last he's responding to the . . . the security I can offer him.'

Brian made no reply to this. Instead, he pulled her towards him, looked deep into her eyes, then slid his arms about her. In the corridor outside, Frank had remembered something. He stopped by Julia's door. Inside, about to kiss, Brian and Julia heard his voice: 'Hang on – shan't be a minute.' The door handle turned.

Brian hurled himself across the room, scooped up the telephone. A little breathlessly he said, 'Now, don't be so crass, Morgan . . .' With an almost furtive little wave, he greeted Frank.

'Have you got the paper on Ibsen?' Frank asked Julia. He thought she looked very bright-eyed and pink-cheeked for a girl usually so sallow. She really was very attractive. He tried to remember when they'd last made love. From behind him came Brian's commercial chatter.

'No, I'm not presenting you with an ultimatum, Morgan. But still, I think . . .'

Julia found the paper on a side table and gave it to him. 'What's it for?' she asked.

'Thanks. It's for my O.U. student.'

'Oh, yes . . . *What*'s her name?'

Frank told her and she nodded, remembering. 'When are we going to meet her?' she asked. 'She sounds fun. Why don't you invite her for supper?'

The idea took Frank aback – Rita belonged in his study, not his house. He stammered a noncommittal reply; even as he did so, he recognised the idea as a good one. Yes, invite Rita, show her off a little, give her the chance to shine, give her a foretaste of the world she wanted to enter. Yes, why not? Invite Rita . . .

'Thanks for the paper,' he said moving towards the door.

Brian said into the telephone, 'Yes . . . yes. All right.'

Frank pointed a thumb at him. 'Doesn't he possess a phone?' he asked.

Brian, with a firm 'Goodbye,' put down the receiver. 'Hello, Frank,' he said. He took a step or two towards where Frank stood by the door, ready to leave, but still watching him. 'Frank, I think you should know . . .' Glancing at Julia, he saw the terror in her eyes and realised, with a start of surprise, that her fear echoed his own. 'I think you should know that . . . er . . . I'm going to change my publisher.'

Frank nodded, smiled. His heavy-lidded eyes seemed to Brian for the first time sinister. Was Frank perhaps a dangerous man? 'I'm glad to hear it,' said Frank. 'That should help my phone bill considerably.' He walked from the room.

Brian drew a deep breath, cleared his throat. He felt oddly diminished. He took a step towards Julia, but she drew back.

'I think you ought to go now,' she said.

He nodded, walked slowly to the door. There he turned, drew himself up. 'I meant everything I said, Julia.' Pomposity mingled with sincerity in his tones. 'Every word.' He followed Frank out into the corridors that ran through the university buildings like shafts through a mine.

Frank, crossing the court towards the door of his staircase, heard from behind him the clatter of running feet. He turned to face the oncoming Rita. 'Form squares!' he commanded himself. 'Stand firm!' Even from a distance he could see the petulance in her expression.

'Forster!' she called out, approaching. 'This friggin' Forster!' He turned and they walked on side by side. 'I'll tell you what Forster does. He gets on my tits!'

'Good. You must show me the evidence.'

She stared up at him, round-eyed. 'You dirty sod!' Then she laughed. The pink tinge, he noticed, had vanished from her hair. Her clothes were more sober than he remembered – dark blouse, blue skirt – a restrained ensemble, he thought, might be the description. Was our Rita beginning to change?

They climbed the stairs. 'That Forster – I just can't understand what he's on about. It's no good, Frank – when it comes to him, I've got a blank. I just can't understand.'

Frank heaved the door of his study open – Rita's oil hadn't helped much. He crossed to his desk, and began to take papers out of his briefcase.

'It's all right for you,' Rita was saying behind him, 'but I just can't figure it.'

He smiled at her. 'You will, you will,' he said. 'But d'you think we could forget about Forster for a moment?'

'With pleasure,' she said tartly.

Frank held up a piece of paper, waving it gently in her face. 'I want to talk to you about this that you sent me. All right? . . . In response to the question, "Suggest how you would resolve the staging difficulties inherent in a production of Ibsen's *Peer Gynt*," you have written – quote – "Do it on the radio." Unquote.' They looked at each other in a silence that seemed to both of them more than long enough. 'Well?' he asked at last.

'Well what?' Her eyes gleamed defiance.

'Well, I know it's probably quite naive of me, but I did think you might let me have a considered essay.'

She felt beset, unfairly harassed. On the other hand, he had a point. He had a right to expect her to work. 'That's all I could do in the time.' He looked unconvinced. She added, 'We were dead busy in the shop this week.'

'You write your essays at work?'

She hesitated. Was this a can of worms she wanted to open now – or ever? She shrugged. 'Yeah,' she said. 'Denny gets dead narked if I work at home. He doesn't like me doin' this – and I can't be bothered arguin' with him.'

Not for the first time when talking to Rita, Frank felt that he'd been wrong-footed. Nevertheless, he had truths to point out. 'Rita, you can't go on producing work as thin as this. At least, not if you want to pass any exams.'

Sensing a weakness, Rita fought back. 'I thought it was the right answer. I sort of . . . encapsulated all me ideas in one line.'

'Rita, it's the basis for an argument – but one line is hardly an essay. You know that as well as I do.'

Did she know that as well as he did? Did she know it at all? She glowered at him, apparently not prepared to give an inch. Suddenly, she snatched the paper from him. In a gesture remembered down the urchin generations since World War II, she stuck a finger under her nose in a parody of a Hitler moustache. With a sneer, she snapped her heels together, flung her arm up in a Nazi salute, then goose-stepped across the room to the other desk. As she sat down, she looked at him again, a dark-eyed, scowling look that promised some unspeakable vengeance. Then she whipped her head round, dismissing him, and bent over her notebook.

As she wrote, he began to sort out essays that were lying on his desk. So quickly did she return, that it was a moment or two before he noticed that she was standing beside him. She was holding out a piece of paper.

'I've done it,' she said.

He looked at her, then at the paper. Almost gingerly he took it from her and read what she'd written. 'In attempting to resolve the staging difficulties in a production of Ibsen's *Peer Gynt*, I would present it on the radio because, as Ibsen himself says, he wrote it as a play for voices, never intending it to go on in a theatre. If they had had a radio in his day, that is where he would have done it.' When he'd read this to himself, he read it aloud. He then sat for quite a long time, looking slowly from Rita to her paper and back again. He sighed. It was clear that, before Rita wrote satisfactory essays, the entire concept of essay-writing would have to be explained to her; what was more important, she would have to accept it. He sighed again. In front of him, he felt, there stretched a long and demanding struggle. He looked at Rita again. The struggle, he thought, would be worth it. 'The idea, as we've agreed, is interesting. Now, let's see whether we can develop it, take it further. And let's see whether it might cause us any difficulties, and what those might be. At the same time, let's consider whether some alternative approach might offer us advantages. All right?'

The gleam in her eyes seemed a hopeful sign. She nodded, a little grimly. They began to work.

But nobody inhabited a life entirely on their own – not even Rita. Frank Bryant had taken over a tiny corner of it, but her husband, Denny, was in imperial possession of measureless sections. If asked, he might have said that he owned all of it: certainly, that he had a traditional male right to do so. Wives belonged to their husbands. That's what Denny had learned while still a small boy, and little he'd seen since had led him to change his mind. It had been a piece of bewildering bad luck for him to have married a woman who had become eager to educate herself, to try to discover what sort of a person she really was. He didn't yet know just how bad his luck had been – but he was shortly to find out.

While his wife continued her struggle to improve her mind, Denny was continuing his to improve their house. In the backyard, a noxious little fire was consuming the debris that, load by load, he was carrying out of the interior. When he'd cleared the worst of the chaos he had created, he clambered to the top of a pair of steps and began to plaster over the scars left by his demolition of the connecting wall.

As he worked, a piece of loose wire caught his attention. It hung down from above, snaking and looping out of the cavity between the ceiling and the next floor. He tried to push it back from below, but its reptilian coils resisted him. With a sigh, he climbed down the steps and went up to the bedroom. His lips pursed, he stood in the doorway, trying to estimate from what precise spot under the floorboards the wire hung. Finally, he made his decision, hauled the carpet aside, and tried one board, then another. The third one lifted. Lying down, he pushed his arm deep into the cavity below, groped for a moment, then smiled as he found what he sought. Swiftly he pulled the wire into place.

It was while he was withdrawing his arm that he found Rita's hidden store of contraceptive pills.

Like a man struck by an instant catalepsy, he knelt motionless on the floor, his eyes fixed on the packet. His mind tried without success to grasp the violation of order that the pills represented. His wife had disobeyed him. His wife had deceived him. His wife had proved to be an unnatural woman, a woman who resisted motherhood. His wife was denying him the children, the *sons*, who would give purpose to his life. These thoughts, half-formed, whirled about his brain, mixed in with fury, self-pity, and visions of vengeance.

After a long time, he got to his feet. But what was he to do? Helplessly, he sat down on the bed, the pills squeezed in his fist. He didn't know how many hours he'd sat there when at last he heard Rita/Susan coming home. He looked up: night had fallen. In the dark bedroom he tried to imagine her movements: her new, jaunty walk; the little smile on her face which, once special for him, now drove him to fury; the bag on her shoulder, bulging with hatefully incomprehensible books. He heard her call him, but he didn't move. She walked into the half-completed lounge, and he could hear the books as – one, two, three, four – they thumped onto the table. A chair scraped – she'd settled down to read them. He felt as though he might burst into tears. Very slowly and cautiously, like a thief in his own house, he got to his feet. Rita, hunched over the table, was deeply absorbed in Chekhov's *The Seagull*. As she read, she tore hunks out of a loaf beside her and pushed them into her mouth, chewing them unbuttered. She had her elbows on the table and her head in her hands. Her hair gleamed in the light. For the moment, her own life had vanished: pre-Revolutionary Russia claimed her.

The pills dropped beside her like a bomb into an idyll. With a gasp, she whirled round. Denny, his face pale, his lips thinned by fury, stood behind her. They looked into each other's eyes without speaking. Chaotic challenges, appeals, accusations and farewells seemed to pass across that frozen silence. Then Rita, drawing a shaky breath, attempted a smile.

'Denny,' she said – but even as she made the attempt she knew that they'd gone beyond explanations. 'Denny, I don't want to have a baby. Not till I've discovered meself.' She wondered if what she'd said had any meaning at all for her husband.

Denny hadn't even heard her. Reaching forward, he scooped up her books, gathered them into his arms. He moved off with them, towards the door. Rita, who'd watched mesmerised, now leaped to her feet. She ran after him, caught him in the doorway. She grabbed his arm, tried to tear loose his hold on the books. His face contorted, he swung his elbow back, struck her high on the chest with his forearm. She tumbled backwards, slid down the wall. Denny marched on, making for the kitchen and the door into the yard.

Whimpering, with fury rather than fear, Rita scrambled to her feet again. She ran into the kitchen, and tried to haul him back by his shirt. He turned to face her and, taking a small step backwards, she began to hit him with her hard, tightly-clenched little fists. Without making a sound, he butted her away with his shoulder, then with another blow of his arm, felled her a second time. Still on the kitchen floor, she heard the door slam behind him.

After a little while, she stood up. She drew a few unsteady breaths, but didn't cry. She walked over to the window. Outside, Denny was skilfully reviving his bonfire, looking for the moment like any other busy householder. Then, one by one, he threw her books into the flames. As she watched, she saw the cover of *The Seagull* twist and curl as though in an agony of its own. She still

42

shed no tears. Expressionlessly, she stood by the window. She felt, even if she didn't know, that she was witnessing one of the abiding images of tyranny's hatred of knowledge. She knew, even if she didn't yet feel, that an entire phase of her life was dying.

*   *   *   *

Frank Bryant looked out of his study window and smiled. The smile was not one of unalloyed joy. What the hell, he wondered to himself, was she playing at? As he looked down at Rita, huddled on a bench facing the university, he realised that this had been a recurrent question in the weeks of their association. Once again he smiled that tight, wry smile. He walked back to his desk, hesitated a moment, then with a sigh walked from the room.

Rita had not moved. Approaching her, he thought that she was looking pale, a little peaky. Perhaps she was sickening for a cold. Her shoulders were hunched, her head forward, her eyes staring expressionlessly at the ground a few feet in front of her. As she became aware of him, she looked up. He expected a smile, some animated excuse, but instead she simply turned her head silently away.

'Hello,' he said. Rita made no answer. He sighed again. 'What's wrong?' This time she shrugged, still not looking up. His look of incipient sympathy faded. 'You know, this is getting to be a bit wearisome. When you come here, Mrs White, you'll do anything except start work immediately. Come on!' She made no move, didn't give him so much as a glance for a reply. He sat down beside her and for a moment they remained like that, silently on the bench. 'Rita, where's your essay?' he asked at last.

'I haven't got it.'

'You haven't done it?'

'I said I haven't *got* it.'

'I see.' He nodded, beginning to feel exasperated. 'Don't tell me – it's been stolen! Whilst you were asleep a gang of Cambridge dons broke into your house and stole your essay on Chekhov!'

He expected some reaction – irritation, perhaps, or one of her long, crowing exclamations: 'Go on!' But she said nothing, simply sat as she had been all along, bowed and white-faced on the bench beside him. He narrowed his eyes, concerned and curious. 'Look, Rita . . .' he began, but she cut him off.

With a sudden fierceness, she said, 'It's burnt!'

'What?'

'So are all the Chekhov books you lent me . . . Denny found out I was on the Pill. He burnt all me books.'

'Oh, Christ!' said Frank. He felt as though he'd suddenly, and for the first time, been dropped into the mean reality of her life. He'd never understood, he told himself, all that she'd been up against.

'I'm sorry,' Rita was saying, 'I'll buy you some more books.'

'Sod the books! I wasn't referring to the books.'

Again they sat in silence, he now looking as unhappy as she. He felt helpless. All he could offer her was the fact of his existence, of the university's existence – a sort of cultural counter-force that might stand against the other influences in her life.

'Why can't he just let me get on with learnin'?' she asked after a while. 'You'd think I was havin' an affair, the way he behaves.'

The word landed in Frank's mind like a grenade – though not one, he felt, that was really likely to explode. He'd pushed aside any awareness of Rita as sexually desirable – partly because she clearly had no such perception of him. 'Too bloody old,' he said to himself. Nevertheless, he gave the unexploded bomb a dangerous little nudge with his toe, rolling it on in another direction. 'Perhaps, in a way, you *are* having some sort of affair.'

This time her contemptuous crow did answer him. 'Go away! I'm not! What time have I got for an affair? I'm busy enough findin' meself, let alone findin' someone else. I've begun to find *me* – and it's great!' Her eyes were shining now, she seemed to be expanding as the energy began throbbing again within her. 'It is, you know, Frank. It might sound selfish, but all I want for the time bein' is what I'm findin' inside me. I certainly don't want to be rushin' off with some feller. 'Cos the first thing I'd have to do is forget about me for the sake of him.'

Frank nodded, a little moodily. He couldn't prevent himself from prodding that grenade again, a little more dangerously than before. 'Perhaps,' he murmured, 'perhaps your husband thinks you're having an affair with me.' The thought was both familiar and very strange, both terrifying and enticing.

Raucously, she dismissed it. 'Oh, go away! You're me teacher. I've told him.'

'You've told him about me?' He considered this, hearing his name bandied about in that house where books had been burned. 'What did you say?'

'I . . . I've tried to explain to him – how you give me room to breathe. You just, like, feed me . . . without expectin' anything in return.'

He tried to keep his face expressionless. He felt breathless, as though he'd just been punched. Her honesty was transforming him: in time he might even become the person she saw. 'What did he say?' he asked.

'He didn't.' She paused, frowning down at the ground. 'I said to him, "You soft get! Even if I was havin' an affair, there's no point burnin' me books. I'm not havin' an affair with Anton Chekhov".' She shook her head, gave a little smile. 'He said, "I wouldn't put it past you to shack up with a foreigner!" '

They sat without speaking. Distant traffic blared and brawled, while around their feet quarrelling sparrows waited misguidedly for crumbs. 'What are you going to do, Rita?' Frank asked eventually.

'Order some new copies and do the essay again.'

'I mean about your husband?'

Ah, she thought – the question she hadn't yet dared to ask. Trust Frank to pose it. That's the academic mind for you. Goes straight to the one important point. She said, 'I told him I'd only have a baby when I had choice. But he doesn't understand. He thinks we've got choice 'cos we can go into a pub that sells eight different kinds of beer. He thinks we got choice already. Choosin' which washing powder. Choosin' between one lousy school and the next, between what lousy jobs there are . . . Choosin' between margarine and butter!'

She looked small, but embattled – both fierce and forlorn at the same time. Frank saw suddenly that she could lose this campaign she'd embarked on; the realisation came as a shock. Nothing in his own life, certainly as he remembered it now, had ever had the fierce importance her education had for Rita. She was involved in a total war, of which the outcome would be either complete triumph or catastrophic defeat. In any case, win or lose, she'd suffer wounds. 'Do you love your husband?' he asked. 'Denny – do you love him?'

In a low voice, she tried for an answer. 'I see him lookin' at me sometimes and I know what he's thinkin'. I do, you know – he's wondering where the girl he married has gone to. He even brings me presents sometimes . . . hopin' the presents'll make her come back. But she can't, because she's gone. And I've taken her place.'

She bowed her head, saying no more. Had she really answered Frank's question? It seemed to her that her reply had been devious, even evasive: she hadn't faced things squarely. She sighed. Perhaps some questions were better evaded. She straightened, smiled at him a little wanly, then rose to her feet. 'Come on,' she said. 'There's always the work.' And she marched off towards his waiting study.

Over the next few weeks, the sessions Frank had with her went smoothly – even, he thought sometimes, rather tamely. Rita, scowling ferociously, now and then rounding on him, her voice wailing argumentatively, now and then sulking, nevertheless began to learn how to fit the workings of her lively mind into a framework acceptable to examiners. Her essays, although still idiosyncratic and personal – unique, Frank thought, marvellously fresh, but utterly non-academic – began to lengthen, to deal with more than one idea at a time and, as her knowledge broadened, to refer to a more acceptable range of books and plays.

As for Rita herself, she felt a little as though she'd thrown herself over a cliff. She had entered an unknown dimension; when she landed, bones might be broken. It wasn't just that she did the work Frank set her. On her own she set out on a High Culture assault course that might have broken lesser spirits. She visited every gallery, every exhibition. The fractured still-lifes of Braque, the brilliance of Matisse, the demanding contortions of Picasso portraits; the dazzle of Op Art, the brashness of Pop Art, the dribblings of Abstract Expressionism, the calm of the New Naturalists, the dreamscapes of Surrealism – Rita saw them all, desperately trying to fit them into an experience of art that had hitherto been confined to advertisements, calendars, chocolate boxes and Christmas cards.

She went to concerts – not only to works of which she'd always been vaguely aware, such as great symphonies of Beethoven and Tchaikovsky, Brahms concertos and Bach and Handel oratorios; but also to modern music, sitting through minimalist scratchings that utterly bewildered her, Schoenbergian dissonances she found excrutiating, an evening of Bliss shot through with exhilarating trumpets, and the baffling silence of Cage, Britten felicities and Birtwhistle puzzles.

She made Frank abruptly aware of these extra-curricular activities one day when he was lecturing to some twenty first-year students. His subject was The Tragic Hero. As he spoke, he glanced now and then out of the large windows of this ground-floor room, as though hoping for rescue. He felt imprisoned – by his task, by the students, above all perhaps by the sound of his own voice, repeating ideas he'd already put forward year after year. They hadn't, he thought wryly, been in any way original in the first place and they'd certainly become pretty shop-soiled since.

The Tragic Hero, he was pointing out, was destroyed by a flaw in his own character. 'This flaw, this . . . er . . . black spot, is the worm – the maggot in an otherwise perfect apple. If we pursue this analogy, we can see the Tragic Hero as a sort of apple, but one in which there is a maggot. So there we have it – the maggot, slowly but relentlessly devouring the apple from within . . .' He droned on – about the nature of evil, external evil and inner evil, about reaction to temptation and the consolidation of a flawed state of mind, the acquisition of a character bound inevitably for wickedness and self-destruction. That, he pointed out, was the Tragic Hero of modernity, as opposed to that of the ancients, who had by some action brought upon himself the inevitable punishment of the gods. 'It is possible to suppose, therefore,' he intoned, 'that Shakespeare's tragedies, as opposed to those of the Greeks . . .'

He looked up, and there stood Rita. His audience had seen her already, and indeed she'd have been hard to miss. She was outside one of the tall windows, crouching forward, gesturing wildly in his direction. She wore the bright pink nylon smock of a hairdresser. Her face was twisted into an expression that he interpreted as furious, perhaps frightened. Embarrassed, he waved an arm at her to indicate that he'd meet her outside the door of the room. He told his students to wait and, irritated and curious, walked out into the hall. He tried to imagine what crisis had brought her: perhaps Denny had threatened her with violence. Worse – perhaps Denny had threatened him with violence!

With a clatter of heels on the marble floor, she came running towards him. 'Frank!' she cried. 'Frank!' Heads turned; there were nudges, giggles. 'Frank, I just had to tell someone!'

'What is it?' Frank asked. He was beginning to be genuinely alarmed. 'What's wrong?'

'Frank, last night . . . last night I went to the theatre!'

He stared at her in total disbelief. 'The theatre! My God, I thought it was something serious.'

'It *was* . . . It was Shakespeare!' She said this as though it was self-explanatory, as though he would instantly

48

understand her excitement.

He disappointed her. In tones of the coldest irritation, he said, 'Rita, I thought something had happened to you.'

'Somethin' did happen to me!' Nothing could cool her enthusiasm. 'Frank, it was fantastic!' She took a copy of *Macbeth* from her bag and began to wave it in his face. She looked like a political fanatic waving a manifesto. 'Look! *Macbeth*, it was. I bought the book. Ooh! It done me head in!' She laughed up at him, still dazzled. And Frank, relaxing, saw that she was possessed by whatever spirit the play had released in her, and overwhelmed by her reactions. She said, 'I thought it was gonna be dead borin' – but it wasn't. It was electric! . . . Wasn't his wife a cow, eh? And that fantastic bit where he meets Macduff and he thinks he's all invincible. I was on the edge of me seat at that bit. I wanted to shout out and tell Macbeth – warn him.'

'You didn't, did you?' He had a clear vision of her, rising from her seat, gesticulating, but she quickly switched that picture off.

'No!' She snorted her denial, taking him seriously; then added explanation: 'They'd have thrown me out the theatre!' He smiled agreement, but Rita had already dismissed the matter. Thoughtfully, she was biting her lip, frowning as she tried to define and place what she'd experienced. '*Macbeth*'s a tragedy, isn't it?' she asked. As Frank smiled and nodded his agreement, she gave a deep sigh, looking up at him like someone waking from deep sleep. Suddenly, she looked dismayed. 'Well . . .' she said. He saw that she'd become self-conscious, aware that she'd burst uninvited into his day. 'Well, I just . . . I just had to tell someone who'd understand.'

'I'm honoured that you chose me,' said Frank. And he was – honoured and touched and gratified.

Rita, beginning to back away, smiled feebly. 'I'm sorry I disturbed you . . .'

But Frank had seen an opportunity. He moved towards her and took her elbow. He nodded towards the door of the lecture room. 'Why don't you come in and wait for me. I'm

49

just finishing off.' Rita's eyes widened in alarm. She leaned back, resisting him; he felt like a parent trying to persuade a reluctant child into school. Firmly, he marched her forward. 'Come on – you'll find it interesting.'

Blank-faced with terror, Rita stepped over the threshold. This was the real university, these the real students. The Open University was a non-place, a dream, amorphous, unfocused, in which she was in essence the only student and Frank the only teacher. Lecturers spoke comfortingly from the familiar television screen; one watched programmes, one didn't attend seminars. Education became a sort of hobby, a simple extension of ordinary life. But here was a different reality: an actual room, an audience of accepted students, flesh-and-blood, ready to judge her, ready to jeer at her if she made a mistake, people of wide reading and swift vocabulary who'd see at once that she was a fraud. Holding herself very stiffly, looking neither right nor left, she walked to the place Frank had indicated and sat down in it. Her legs felt weak; sweat lay on her upper lip.

Frank smiled at her, then looked around the room. 'Mrs White is on another course, but she's joining us for the rest of this tutorial.' He walked back to his place on the low dais, glanced around at the students again. Still terror-struck, Rita stared at him. What if he was no good, after all? She'd never seen him teach anyone but her. What if, exposed up there, he turned out to be incompetent, a bumbler, losing his way, stammering? . . .

'Now, where were we?' said Frank, then nodded sharply. 'Yes – tragedy . . . We must never confuse tragedy – the tragedy of drama – with the merely tragic. The tragic event, unlike Tragedy, is not marked by inevitability. If we take a tragic hero – Macbeth, for instance . . .'

Rita, watching him stroll slowly to and fro on the dais, had relaxed. No one had taken the slightest real notice of her, Frank was fluent, competent – and he was talking to her, for her: it was because of her, surely, that he'd introduced Macbeth. She leaned forward, intent on what he was saying.

50

'If we accept, then, that Macbeth's character is flawed by his ambition, we see also that it's this flaw in his character which forces him inevitably to take the steps that lead him to his doom. Whereas the sort of thing we read in the newspapers as being tragic – er, "Man Killed by Falling Tree", say – is never in fact a *tragedy* . . .'

Rita by now had entirely recovered herself. 'It is for the poor sod under the tree!' she said crisply. She meant it; when some of the students around her laughed, she turned and glared at them. 'What you laughin' at?' she demanded, hunched as though ready to do battle.

Hastily, Frank took up her point. 'It's tragic, yes – absolutely tragic. But it's not a tragedy – not in the way that *Macbeth*, for example, is a tragedy . . . Now, why is that?'

Characterisation, said the students. Psychological insight, they added. Universality, said one; the poetic dimension, thought another. The inevitable corruption of power, a third pointed out, while his friend perceived a fundamental critique of feudalism and of the idea of a natural ruling class. There was the clever girl who saw 'a paradigm of the male-female interaction, with its inevitable outcome in destruction and death'. There was the man at the back who regarded it as 'tragic because of its historical perspective, its concealed subject being the corruption and degeneration of Queen Elizabeth's father, Henry VIII'.

'I wish I could think like they do,' Rita, silenced, thought to herself – and said so, later, to Frank, as they walked slowly across the university lawns.

Frank, who knew how derivative most of the students' opinions really were, only smiled wryly. 'It's really quite easy,' he said, but knew it wasn't, yet, for her.

'I just thought it was a dead excitin' story, *Macbeth*,' she muttered, almost sullenly. 'But you lot – you see all sorts of things in it, don't you?' She pondered this for a moment, then sighed, smiled. 'It's fun, tragedy, isn't it?'

She walked on silently, brooding again as she watched the students who sat or lounged on the grass around them. She saw them as a group inexplicably favoured – they'd been picked out by a process that as yet didn't seem entirely clear to her, and had been initiated into mysteries. As a result, they had knowledge – not the knowledge Frank and the Open University could give her, but that which preceded it and acted as its base, its foundation. They knew what all the things she was learning meant, they understood how those things fitted together. They'd read enough, talked and listened enough, been around educated people enough, to have gained, almost without trying to, a framework into which all their new discoveries could be placed. Rita, her mind still a chaos of half-understood fragments, felt sometimes that everyone else had learned a code that had been denied her. They could decypher the world's messages, while she could only read them, baffled, certain that they contained an essential element that she would always miss. She felt an overwhelming longing to be supplied as they were with the necessary framework, the necessary code. She hadn't yet realised, as Frank had from the beginning, that frameworks are also cages and that code-books make clear only those cyphers to which they apply.

Abruptly, Frank said, 'Rita, look – how about lunch?'

She stared at him aghast, her eyes wide with horror. 'Christ!' she yelled. 'Me customer!' She indicated her bright pink smock. 'She only wanted a demi-wave. She'll come out lookin' like a friggin' Muppet!'

She turned to run, but Frank grabbed her by the upper arm. 'Rita, what do you do on Saturdays?'

Trying to tug herself free, she said, 'I work.'

'When you finish work?'

Rita stopped struggling and looked at him warily. She'd heard this sort of line before. 'I dunno,' she said, cautiously. What was Frank after?

'I want you to come over to the house.'

'Why?'

'Julia's organised a few people to come round for dinner.'

Bewildered, Rita stared at him. First there had been her invitation into his lecture, now this. At the beginning he'd kept her studies in a clearly marked compartment. Then

52

Denny and her home life had thundered through its boundaries, and now Frank was chipping away at those defences that remained. What was he trying to do? Show her how far she still had to come? Demonstrate that she was kidding herself, that she simply hadn't the background, the poise, the vocabulary – the bloody intelligence, for Christ's sake! – to fulfil her dream? 'You want *me* to come?' she asked finally. Her eyes looked like those of a startled deer; at any second now she would flee. 'Why? Why do you want me to be there?'

Exasperated, Frank said, 'Why do you think?'

But she couldn't think – that was the trouble. 'I dunno.'

'Because you might enjoy it!' It was an aspect of the matter she hadn't considered. She didn't believe that she'd enjoy it, or that whether she would or not had any bearing on the question. 'Will you come?' Frank asked again.

'If you want.' She sounded like a sulky child.

Frank was determined to get through to her, to reach the truth of what she felt. 'What do *you* want?'

To run away, she thought. Not to be faced by problems like this, not to add to the confusion in her life. 'All right,' she said. 'I'll come.'

But Frank hadn't finished. 'Will you bring Denny?'

Denny! She could see him, with his flash smile and crass opinions, spreading himself, beer in hand, at Frank Bryant's dinner table. Julia's dinner table. 'I don't know if he'll come,' she said. But of course she knew he wouldn't.

'Well, ask him,' Frank commanded.

'All right,' she said, almost meekly. She gave a wan smile and turned away. As she began to trot down the path, hastening out of one world and into another, she felt disorientated, totally confused. Too much was being asked of her, she thought. She couldn't cope with as much as this. Why didn't people leave her alone? Why didn't Frank leave her alone to go forward at her own pace? But he wouldn't and now everything was going out of control. Things were happening too fast; it was as though someone had tied a rope around her and was jerking her forward at a greater and greater speed. But it was she herself, she knew, who'd tied on the rope. Only now someone else had caught hold of the other end, and was pulling and heaving . . .

She stopped abruptly. She saw herself, slight, pale and covered in blancmange pink, reflected in a shop window. 'Sweet Jesus!' she said to herself. 'What am I goin' to wear?'

Before she faced that problem, she had to face Denny. 'I wouldn't be seen dead with that lot!' he said; and 'Why the hell should I spend an evening with a bunch of toffee-nosed gets like that?'; and, 'Just because you've gone off your bleedin' head doesn't mean I have to as well.' Wearily, she went upstairs. She tried something formal, mouthed to herself in the mirror, took it off. A black dress brightened by a dash of sequins was viewed, then discarded. A peasant blouse and flowered skirt joined the pile. For a while she paraded up and down in a pale yellow jump suit, but decided finally that it looked too casual. She tried jersey and jeans, a green woollen dress, a pale pink suit. Increasingly, her reflected image distressed her: she looked plain, common, uninteresting. She imagined Frank's dining room, made gorgeous by the beautiful, the brilliantly dressed, the outrageous and the colourful. Christ, she was drab! Boring!

'Boring!' she said to the mirror. 'Boring, boring!'

When she came down at last she was wearing a loose blue shirt over skin-tight blue trousers. Ankle-length boots tap-tapped upon the stairs. Like a tiny echo, rain flung against the windows. She pulled on a coat and picked up her umbrella. She put her head into the sitting room. Denny sat four-square before the television set. On the screen, footballers ran furiously, collided with each other, gesticulated; four in a group leaped for a high ball and missed, while the commentator's voice gibbered in artificial hysteria. All the time, Denny's back faced her, eloquent in its immobility.

'Are you gonna change your mind?' She couldn't afford not to give him every chance.

'No,' said Denny. He didn't turn round.

She felt responsible; in some way, his solitude touched her. 'What will you do?'

'I'm goin' down the pub with your mum and dad. That's where *you* should be goin'.'

On the screen, a bunch of players in bright yellow shirts angrily surrounded the referee. He was waving a little book and shouting. Unseen crowds shouted louder. The commentator shouted loudest of all. With a little grunt of annoyance, Rita began to close the door.

'But we're not good enough for you now, are we?' Denny called savagely over his shoulder.

Rita pulled the door to and marched to the front door. She was already in the act of opening it when she stopped, took a deep breath, then quietly closed it. She walked back to where Denny was sitting. He was watching a man in black and white stripes kicking one of the men in yellow viciously on the shins. The ball, unattended, bobbed along beside them.

Rita said, 'Look, Denny, he invited both of us . . . Go on, change your mind. Come with me.' She waited. Immobile, wordless, Denny watched a man in yellow slide through the mud on his back, his outstretched legs reaching vainly for the ball. 'Come on,' she coaxed, 'you might actually like him.'

Denny turned round. His face was twisted with spite, his voice a falsetto parody of an upper class accent. 'Oh, might I actually, Susan? Isn't that actually, actually nice!' He swung away, bending forward as though fascinated by the brawling figures on the screen.

'Well, fuck you!' Rita/Susan yelled suddenly. She went out, slamming the door behind her. A moment later she was in the rain, almost ready to weep with anger, frustration and a kind of terror. She felt her old life slipping away, a new one out of reach. In the gap between she would be swallowed up, drowned, swept away.

Still distracted by her thoughts, she walked into an off-licence. She'd be expected to bring wine – she was sure of that. But the rows of bottles dismayed her. Their labels proclaimed her ignorance. *Croze-Hermitage*, *Niersteiner Bernkastler*, *Bardolino* – these were snatches of an alien language, the vocabulary of those she had a passion to join, the vocabulary of the educated, the socially secure, the knowledgeable and accepted. It was not a vocabulary she had learned. The words swam before her: *Pomerol*, *Piesporter*, *Pouilly-Fuissé* – the terms of an indictment. Their obscurity defined a denial, since they were not obscure to others. She had been rejected, she felt, in a way she could never overcome, for it had been done without malice or cruelty. She had simply run foul of the natural order of things. She bought a bottle of Spanish red and, carrying it under her arm as furtively as though she had stolen it, rushed out once more into the rain.

Beginning to shiver with cold in the damp wind, she sheltered under a railway bridge. A taxi appeared, its light an invitation. One foot off the kerb, she waved at it frantically. It plunged past as though to emphasise her insignificance – the social order was fixed and would not relent. 'Oh, God,' she thought, 'it's really not my night!' She began to trot along pavements covered with a slime of mud.

By the time she caught a bus going in the right direction, despair lay in her as cold and heavy as a slab of concrete. She felt weighed down by it; it pressed against her stomach, squeezed her lungs, became a burden to her heartbeat. She closed her eyes, praying wordlessly that in the end everything would go all right, that she wouldn't be too late, that she wouldn't look out of place, that she wouldn't make a fool of herself. When she opened her eyes again, she saw that the bus was just sailing past her stop. Yelling, she leaped to her feet. Bus, driver, conductor, passengers – all remained unmoved by her distress. Cursing loudly, she splashed down into the street a third of a mile further on.

Half crying, she began to run through the rain. Passing cars flung muddy spray across her path. Several times her hurrying feet plunged into puddles. Water began to seep through her raincoat. Her hair, bedraggled, hung about her neck and ears. The paper round the bottle turned to pulp. Panting, desperate, she ran on in what now seemed an endless marathon. Its only outcome, she knew, would be disaster.

Railings. Calm trees. Quiet. The pale façades of gracious buildings. Then lights. Gasping for breath, Rita clung to Frank Bryant's gate and looked in at the party that awaited her. Christ, everybody looked so calm! She could see groups of people, glasses in hand, talking with animation, pleased with each other – pleased with themselves. They smiled a great deal, gesticulated and sipped their drinks. She knew those people – they belonged in films, in commercials, in advertisements; she'd seen them in the glossy magazines bought for her clients at the hairdressers'. They weren't people one just walked in and joined. Her only link with them was Frank . . . but wasn't Frank in the end one of them? He'd be on their side. She'd walk into the room and they'd turn and look at her and there she'd be, defenceless, friendless. She could hear her voice, trying to find the right words, falling into sly little conversational traps, making too much noise, turning her into someone ridiculous . . . Good God, she *was* someone ridiculous!

She walked up to the porch of the house. From her handbag she took a little notepad and a pencil and began to scribble. As she wrote, she didn't see how Frank came to the window and looked anxiously out into the night. Even if she had, she wouldn't have believed that he was looking for her. She tore the note from the pad and walked down to where Frank's car was parked beside the steps. She glanced once at the message she'd scribbled: *Sorry. Couldn't come. Rita.* Then she pushed it under a windscreen wiper and walked out through the gate. By the time she emerged into lamplight, Frank had turned from the window again. Rita, looking up at the lights within, hesitated one moment longer. Bending down, she carefully stood the bottle beside the iron fence. Then, straightening, she began to walk decisively away. Under the windscreen wiper, the falling rain began to dissolve the scribbled letters of her message.

She arrived home wet, bedraggled, defeated. The house was empty: its silence both suited her mood and depressed her further. She felt trapped, without the energy or intelligence to escape her fate. In a faded blue dressing-gown and with a towel wrapped around her head, she wandered smoking from room to room. Despite everything, Denny had been right – this was her proper arena. She belonged here, in these narrow rooms, in a small house on an insignificant street. Everything else was dreams. It was Denny and his friends who defined the world she lived in, not Frank Bryant and his lot. It was what she'd been brought up to, what all her friends had settled for. Denny was right to feel rejected and bewildered. Suddenly she longed to feel his arms around her, to be pressed against the warm strength of his chest, to have his hands caress her. She wanted him to make love to her and change everything back to what it had been at the beginning.

She found Denny at the Bierkeller. Grinning with huge delight, he beckoned to her as she hesitated by the door. Beside him sat her father and mother, he red faced, bellowing out the pub songs that by now everyone was singing. Her mother sat next to him, her lips moving stiffly, rather as they did in church. Denny, eyes sparkling, waved a beer-mug as he, too, sang with the rest. The sound beat at Rita as she crossed the room, hammering into her like breakers on a rock. The thick smoke that hung on the air stung her eyes. She realised that she was seeing too much – men half asleep, others unsteady, the rest raucous, their eyes vacant, their mouths agape. She saw the dirt on the floor, the beer-puddled tables, the ashtrays piled with stubs. She saw the peeling paint, the faded prints and posters on the wall, the battered chairs. Everything was second-rate, imitation, empty: even the name of the place had been borrowed from some other place with a different way of doing things. Once she'd enjoyed all this, she reminded herself: she'd thought it a bit of fun, a bit of relaxation – and that was what it was. It hadn't changed, after all. But she had; it wasn't fun for her any more. Frank had offered her an alternative and she'd fled from it: she'd felt just as wrong outside his house as she did now, sitting with Denny and her parents.

Denny put his arm around her and squeezed her shoulder. She leaned against him, but she felt a fraud. Even sitting there, she was deceiving him: she wasn't there in the sense he thought she was. She felt alien, distant, like a stranger who'd come to observe the strange antics of the natives. She felt absent from herself as much as from Denny and the others. Looking around, she realised she was frightened. She had stumbled out into some terrible no man's land, some area of the mind, of life, in which there was no one to help or support her. She was in a limbo between worlds and nothing now would ever have the power to lead her home again.

She watched without surprise as down her mother's long, pale cheeks silent, beery tears began to flow. Around them the bellowing rolled on; but the two women sat in their own stillness, the younger with her head turned, observing apparently without emotion the terrible, noiseless weeping of the older.

It seemed to both of them a long time before Rita leaned forward and asked, 'Why are you crying, mother?'

Her mother went on weeping for a moment without speaking. Then she sighed, the exhalation long and shaky. She said, 'There must be better songs to sing than this.'

Perhaps if that sentence hadn't continued to resound in her mind during the days that followed, Rita would never have gone back to the university, and to Frank Bryant and his battered study. But somehow it was a statement that not only seemed to apply to her, but was also one that she wanted to share with Frank. She wanted his opinion on it. Some part of her had resolved before this that the Open University and all it implied was not for her. Yet, with her mother's words still echoing about her head, and with both habit and a natural stubbornness putting her on automatic pilot, she found herself once more climbing those stairs and pushing her way past the door's resistance into the familiar room.

But she returned only to discover Frank in a towering and uncharacteristic fury. ' "Sorry, couldn't come. Rita" ', he quoted savagely. 'Of course you could have come!' He marched to and fro, white faced. 'Certainly you could have come!'

'I couldn't!' Rita snapped back. She too felt angry. She'd

59

been through enough. 'I couldn't!'

'Why?'

She faced him, quivering, desperate. 'I couldn't – I'd brought the wrong kind of wine!'

The very absurdity of this proclaimed her despair. Brought up short, Frank looked at her without speaking for a moment. He saw for the first time how tired she looked, and how strained. 'Rita,' he said, quietly now, 'for Christ's sake . . . I wanted *you* to come. You weren't expected to . . . to dress up or buy wine.'

Bitterly she replied with a question. 'If you go out to dinner, don't you dress up? Don't you buy wine?'

'Yes. But . . .' He stared at her, helplessly. He had put her in a special category of her own – but then that's where she belonged. Was it patronising to recognise that? Certainly, he knew, it would sound patronising if he tried to explain it.

'Well?'

'Well, what?'

'Well . . .' She gave a little shrug; a gesture of disillusion. 'You wouldn't take sweet, sparkling wine, would you?'

'Does it matter what I do? It wouldn't have mattered if you'd walked in with a bottle of Spanish plonk.' But with a sinking heart he saw her swift change of expression – he'd blundered.

'It *was* Spanish,' she said, her voice icy.

They faced each other as though frozen by her cold anger – her hatred for me, thought Frank, and her contempt for herself. He realised, as though he hadn't seen her for a long time, how much she'd changed. Her hair had altered: it was less elaborate, and surely longer? And her clothes were plainer, darker, altogether more restrained. She really was in the process of a transition. It was one, he knew, that was bound to be difficult and painful. She needed all the help she could get.

'Why couldn't you relax?' he asked at length. 'It wasn't a fancy dress party. You could have come as yourself . . . Don't you realise how people would have seen you if you'd just breezed in?' He smiled, while she looked up at him, stone faced. 'They'd have seen someone who's funny, delightful, charming . . .'

She cut him off. 'I don't wanna be charming and delightful,' she shouted. 'Funny? What's funny? I don't wanna be funny! I wanna talk seriously with the rest of you. I don't wanna spend the night takin' the piss . . . comin' on with the funnies because that's the only way I can get into the conversation. I didn't wanna come to your house just to . . . just to play the Court Jester!'

'You weren't being asked to play that role. I just wanted you to be yourself.'

Rita shook her head, more as though to clear it than in denial. More quietly now, thinking out what she said, she tried to explain. 'I don't want to be "just myself". Me? What's me? Some stupid woman who gives us all a laugh because she thinks she can learn, because she thinks that one day she'll be like the rest of them, talking seriously, confidently, with knowledge . . . living a civilised life.' Her voice had risen again, whipped up by her frustration and despair. 'Well, she can't be like that really – but bring her in because she's always good for a laugh!'

The obstinacy with which she clung to her devaluation of herself suddenly infuriated Frank. 'If you believe that's why you were invited – to be laughed at – then you can get out now! You were invited because I wished to have your company.'

Again they faced each other in silence. Rita tried once more to explain how she felt. 'Look, I'm all right with you, here in this room. But when I saw those people you were with . . . I couldn't come in. I'd have seized up. Because I'm a freak – I can't talk to the people I live with any more, and I can't talk to the likes of them at your house. I'm a half-caste . . .' Her eyes now on the ground, she told Frank about her visit to the pub. 'And I thought to myself, just what the frig am I tryin' to do? Why don't I just pack it in, stay with them, join in the singin'?'

'And why don't you?'

That was when she looked up at him and told him about her mother's tears. 'You think I still can, don't you?' she

61

said. 'Join in the singin'. Just because you pass a pub doorway and hear that singin' you think we're all okay . . . that
we're all survivin', with the spirit intact . . . But when I
asked me mother why she was cryin', she said, "There must
be better songs to sing than this". And I thought – that's
what I'm tryin' to do, aren't I? Sing a better song . . . And
that's why I came back. And that's why I'm stayin'.'

*   *   *   *

The seasons turned. Autumn came, then winter. The trees
poured out their leaves; snow flurries whitened their
branches. Between Rita and her husband, a sort of truce
was maintained. She straddled her two worlds and managed to survive by keeping them separate. When the
politics of domesticity demanded it, she went out with
Denny, but what amused him seemed to her increasingly
artificial and unsatisfactory. Her life with him felt in some
essential way unreal – yet it remained the only life she had.
It was with him that she ate, planned, slept and made love.
She found the difference between the actualities of her
existence and what she secretly felt about them hard to
bear. Gritting her teeth, she bore them, not knowing what
else to do. The fact that her work as a student was clearly
progressing made her burden easier to bear – at least it now
had a purpose. More and more, though, she caught herself
thinking of her present situation as temporary.

While the snow lay thick on the ground, there was a
wedding – that of Sandra, Rita/Susan's sister. Had she and
her bridegroom been a little less sexually impetuous, they
might have been able to wait for a later, more conventional
season, but pregnancy has its own calendar. Nevertheless,
the family looked happy enough as it lined up, three deep
on the snowy steps, smiling for the necessary photographs.

Rita, in powder-blue, a little round hat setting off her
triangular face, stood next to her father. She stared out at
the camera lens, smiling brightly, doing her best for a cause
in which, she thought, she no longer really believed.

'Well, that's the last of you lot off me hands!' Her father

spoke thickly, as though he'd already taken more than
enough strong drink. Rita glanced sideways, searching for
the bulge of a flask in his pockets. Suddenly he turned his
head to look back at her, his expression blearily ferocious.
'Mind you,' he growled, 'I don't know why some of you
bother gettin' bloody married!'

The photographer called to them and they responded,
grimacing their collective happiness. His lights flashed at
them so that one almost expected a little local thunder.

Knowing very well what he'd meant, Rita asked her
father, 'What's that supposed to mean?'

'Are you still not pregnant?' Denny nudged Rita,
demanding smiles. She stretched lips that felt like plastic:
her face had stiffened in anger. Beside her, her father
returned to his theme. 'How old are you now, Susan?'

Through her tight, unmanageable lips, Rita said,
'Seventy-four!'

He shook his head. He was a thickset man, with a drink-
reddened face and greying hair. He looked as if he'd be
a formidable man in a fight, but less effective in a
conversation. He had little sense of humour, and none at
all to spare for this subject. He shook his head again,
frowning. 'No, you're not – you're twenty-six. Been
married six years, and you've not got a baby to show for it.
Here's your sister – she's only been married two minutes
and she's already four months pregnant!'

Sandra, overhearing, glared at her father. And Rita,
seeing an advantage, snapped, 'Why don't you get on the
air waves and broadcast it?'

'There's nothin' wrong with bein' pregnant before you're
married. Your mother was three months gone when I
married her.'

This time it was his wife who glared at him, both angry
and hurt. Rita said, 'That's what I've always admired in
you, dad – you're just overflowin' with innate sensitivity
and charm!'

Sandra and her new husband were walking away down
the church path. Rita stepped out with the rest of the
family, now straggling after the happy couple. Rita's

63

father, with a half sneer, turned to Denny. 'Eh, Denny, Denny – I feel sorry for you, lad. If she was a wife of mine, I'd drown her.'

Rita came spinning round, her eyes glittering with fury. 'If I was a wife of yours,' she hissed at him, 'I'd drown *meself*!'

She marched off down the path, hearing Denny's angry voice behind her: 'Hey! Hey, that was your father you insulted!' His feet came pounding after her; she could hear him panting with effort and irritation. His hand grasped her arm. She wrenched herself free.

'Oh, sod off!' she cried, and hurried away.

If it hadn't been her sister's wedding, she wouldn't have come back. But she owed it to Sandra to appear at the reception. Arguing herself into a more amenable frame of mind, she joined Denny and the rest in the dusty pub room they'd chosen for the celebration. She stood near the doorway, looking around at the braying uncles, the sweating cousins, the over-excited nieces and nephews. A hired DJ, pretending the hysterics of his trade, was whipping records on and off a turntable: the music he made throbbed through the room. People ate, people drank, people danced; having danced, they drank again and, drinking, they ate. They shouted at each other, trading insults, bad jokes and gossip. The white tiers of the cake rose at one end of the room like a monument – or a gravestone, more like, she thought, marking the dead past.

A half-remembered cousin snatched her away, and she danced. After a while, without quite knowing how, she found herself being twirled to and fro in Denny's strong arms. Shouting through the music, he proclaimed anew his dissatisfactions. Her sister's marriage had made him take a closer look at his own. Hardly listening to the familiar list of his complaints, she almost missed his ultimatum: if she didn't change, they were finished. 'It's dead easy, Susan. You stop goin' to that university and you stop takin' the Pill – or you're out!'

The music blared and beat around them. She thought about what he'd just said. She felt unutterably weary of the entire subject, yet owed her marriage one more rescue attempt. 'Why?' she asked.

'You know why!' an infuriated Denny bawled in her ear.

'I don't, though, Denny. All I'm doin' is gettin' an education. That's all – just tryin' to learn . . . And I love it! It's not easy. I get it wrong most of the time. I'm laughed at half of the time. But I love it – 'cos it makes me feel as though I'm in the land of the livin'. . . . And all *you* ever try and do is put a rope round me neck and tie me to the ground.'

But Denny was many months past the point when he might have listened. Perhaps he'd never reached such a point. His face stubbornly set, he only said, 'Are you gonna pack it in, Susan?'

Suddenly her heart was hammering. Almost without becoming aware of it, she'd stumbled into a crisis that would utterly transform her life. The awareness terrified her: this is how it must be, she thought, when one turned an ignition switch and a bomb went off. She looked him in the eyes. Very slowly and seriously, she shook her head. No, she wouldn't pack it in, not then, not ever.

They stopped dancing. His hands fell away from her. He was very pale. How dark his eyes were! How soft his lips! Without a word, he turned away and walked slowly towards the buffet. The crowd there opened, engulfed him, closed. For a moment longer she stood where she was, almost as though expecting him to come back. But she knew he wouldn't come back. She looked slowly around the room. One marriage begins, another ends. She wanted suddenly to yell out her news, to wipe the easy smugness off the faces around her. But who would understand it, or care? They'd all agree with Denny: serve her right, they'd say. And so it did. Without another glance at any of them, she walked from the room.

By the time Denny came home, Rita had packed what she needed and moved out. She went to the only other home she knew: her parents' house on a council estate at the edge of the city. Despite her mother's timid welcome, she had to settle there in the vast shadow of her father's disapproval. At any moment, she thought, he might tell her

65

to go back to Denny or get out. She kept mostly to her room, the room she and Sandra had shared during her own last, pointless years at school. Now she sat in its dreary quiet, reading the books and writing the essays that Frank set her. In her spare time, she searched frantically for a room nearer the city centre and the university, that she could afford.

Her whole life seemed to her to have become unstable, like a sand-castle faced with an advancing tide. It would all go soft and spongy, sag, crumble, and fall in on itself. It was Frank Bryant who now became the one fixed point in her life. She'd gone to him the day after her final departure from Denny's house. Explaining to him what had happened, she had, to her own intense astonishment, burst into bitter tears.

'He said it's warped me,' she sobbed. 'He said I've betrayed him . . . I suppose I have.' Frank, moving closer, tried to comfort her. He put his hands on her shoulders, but she waved an irritated arm and moved away. 'I'm sorry. It's just . . . You know. I'll be all right. Just give me a minute.' Turning from him, she forced herself to be calm, steadied her breathing and dried her eyes. When finally she'd set her features in their accustomed order, she asked, 'What was me *Macbeth* essay like?'

'Oh, sod *Macbeth*!'

But she wouldn't have any of that, wanting no sympathy from him to swamp and distort their teacher-student relationship. 'No,' she said, harshly. 'No, come on! I want you to tell me what you think about it.'

'In the circumstances . . .' Frank began, but her hard voice stopped him.

'It doesn't matter. It doesn't! . . . In the circumstances I need to go on. I need to talk about the essays, and to do them . . . What was it like? I told you it was no good . . . Is it really useless?'

Frank stared at her in bewilderment. He wanted to comfort her, to heal her wounds. She'd turned to him and he owed her concern, some gentleness. But now she said that she wanted something different – the usual objectivity, the established distance: criticism, discussion, ideas, and no softness. Business as usual. 'I . . . I really don't know what to say.'

'Well, try and think of something! . . . Go on! I don't mind if you tell me it was rubbish.' She waited, then saw that he was still hesitating. 'I don't want pity, Frank,' she said in a lower voice. She smiled wanly up at him. 'Was it rubbish?'

Frank sat down at his desk. Distractedly, his hands shifted papers. 'No,' he muttered, 'no, it's not rubbish.' He looked down at what he was doing, became more purposeful, and a moment later held up her essay. 'Not rubbish at all. It's a totally honest, passionate account of your reaction to the play. It's an unashamedly emotional statement about a certain experience.'

Her lip curled a little. 'Sentimental, eh?'

'No. It's too honest for that. It's almost . . . almost moving. But in terms of what you're asking me to teach you – in terms, that is, of passing exams . . .' He dropped her essay on the desk again and looked at her. To give her what she wanted, as he'd known from the beginning, risk destroying what she already had. To condemn what she had written was dishonest; not the work of a teacher, but of an academic bureaucrat, a man obsessed with exam results rather than true knowledge. He felt unequal to the weight she had laid on him; her demand was not that he should teach her, but turn her into a model student. She *wanted* an academic bureaucrat. He tried to find the right words to explain his dilemma, but heard himself do no more than stammer incoherently. 'Oh, God . . . you see, I . . . I don't . . .'

'Say it!' she cried impatiently. 'Go on! Say it!'

Frank nodded. In a controlled voice he said, 'In those terms, in examination terms, the essay's worthless. It shouldn't be, but it is.' He looked at her, then smiled. 'In its own terms, it's . . . it's wonderful.'

'It's worthless!' Rita's voice remained harsh. She didn't believe his compliments, not understanding that there were two sets of competing values. 'Worthless – *you* said. And if it's worthless, you've got to tell me. Because I wanna write essays like those on there.' She pointed at the piles of paper on his desk, the predictable compilations of acceptable opinion that she held in so much awe. 'I wanna know – and pass exams like they do.'

'But if you're going to write this sort of stuff, you're going to have to change.'

'All right.' She nodded – change was what she wanted. 'Tell me how to do it.'

Frank tried once more to explain his dilemma. But in his heart he knew it was useless and perhaps even dishonest: he already had the knowledge Rita hankered after. That was how he knew its worthlessness. But had he the right to deny it to her? Nevertheless, he said now, 'But I . . . I don't know if I want to tell you. Rita, I don't know that I want to teach you. What you already have is valuable.'

'Valuable?' She spat the word. 'What's valuable? The only thing I value is here . . . comin' here once a week.'

'But don't you see, if you're going to write this sort of thing' – he too indicated piled papers – 'and pass examinations, you . . . you're going to have to suppress, perhaps abandon altogether . . . your uniqueness. I'm going to have to change you.'

Rita was exasperated: what the hell was the matter with the man? 'Don't you realise, I *want* to change!' As they glowered at each other, a new suspicion struck her – was this Frank the gentleman, trying to let her down gently? 'Is this your way of tellin' me I can't do it? That I'm not good enough?'

'Of course you're good enough. It's not that at all. I'm just . . .'

'Because if that's what you're tryin' to tell me, I'll go now!'

'No, no, no!' Frank cried. The last thing he wanted was that she should march out, rejected here too. 'Of course you're good enough.'

But Rita had worked out to her own satisfaction what was bothering him. Her waywardness, her apparent vulnerability, her age and class origins, all combined to make her

68

difficult to teach. She smiled – a tight, humourless smile, but she intended it as reassurance. She said, 'See, it's difficult for you with someone like me. But you've gotta keep tellin' me, and then I'll start to take it in. You see, with me you've got to be dead firm. You won't hurt me feelin's, you know. If I do somethin' that's crap, I don't want pity. You just tell me, "That's crap!" ' She grabbed her essay from where it lay in front of him. With a sudden, violent movement, she tore the pages in two. 'Here – it's crap! So we dump that in the bin and start again.'

She flung the remnants in the wastepaper basket by his desk, then marched across to the other and sat down. She took out her notepad, setting out a heading in block letters: *MACBETH*. Bending forward, she began to write.

Later, it became clear to both of them that this precise moment had been the point of Rita's metamorphosis. Perhaps the physical ending of her marriage, which had in reality ended so long before, had released new energies in her. Perhaps it was the choice Frank had by implication laid before her: stay as you are or become a good student. Perhaps it was a natural stage in an evolution that had begun years before. In any case, Rita changed. She took with a deadly seriousness work at which she'd previously done little more than play. She'd fancied the thought of herself as a student; now she became one. She'd delighted in the idea of being knowledgeable; now she began to acquire knowledge. She'd responded with incoherent pleasure to a few of the works to which her course had introduced her, remaining unmoved by the rest; now she responded to all of them with her intellect – an intellect increasingly armed with the weapons of the academic critic.

Thus as the year turned, her own wintry despair began to thaw. She began to blossom with the spring. Frank, watching her develop, set aside his own misgivings. Her increasing success re-established her high spirits, and these seemed to compensate for the increasing strictness of the discipline that limited her work. It was the discipline, of course, that established her success, and so the circle was complete. Within it, she developed a new confidence, much more soundly based and much less brittle than the old. Her astonishment at finding she could do the work Frank set her gave way to a sort of constant glee: she lived with the coming-true of a dream.

With the summer, however, came a new testing of her confidence. Her career as a student had up to now had a particular location: Frank Bryant's study. And it had had a single mentor, a single observer: Frank himself. Now the time had come when she would have to try out her new abilities in a different arena – her name was down for attendance at one of the Open University's summer schools. It was the only chance O.U. students had to work together, to see their screen tutors in the flesh, to attend lectures – to be, for a short while, 'real' students. But as the time for departure grew nearer, Rita became more and more nervous. It seemed to her that once again she was standing on that rainy pavement outside Frank's house, certain that the world within the lighted windows would never be for her. Nevertheless, the moment came when, packed and as ready as she could make herself, she presented herself at Frank's study, her last stop on the way to the station.

He carried her suitcase across the university lawns, stowed it in the luggage compartment of his car, and climbed in beside her.

Terrified, she watched the pavements sweep by, crowded with the careless, the satisfied, the unburdened. 'Frank,' she wailed, 'Frank . . . I don't wanna go!'

'You have to,' he said, simply. There was no more to it than that. She knew it, but felt the need to complain. 'Oh, Frank . . . I wish you were gonna be there. You understand me.'

Frank covered his pleasure at her faith in him with a show of irritation. 'And the tutors at the Summer School will understand you, for God's sake!'

'What if they realise how thick I am?'

Frank gave her the reassurance for which she was angling. 'They won't because you're not . . . Rita, my dear, you can do it now! Just write the sort of essays you've begun

70

to write for me and you'll have nothing to worry about.'

'I still wish you were gonna be there,' she muttered like a sulky child.

He looked at her, hunched on the seat beside him. He was almost swept away by a sudden overwhelming flow of . . . what, exactly? Compassion, he told himself, protectiveness, admiration. 'So do I, Rita,' he said, his voice unexpectedly hoarse. 'So do I.'

At the station, she marched up the platform beside him, her expression that of a prisoner condemned to a long and uncomfortable stretch. Glancing at her, he realised how much she'd changed. Her hair was no longer barmaid blonde, but dark, long and simple. Her clothes, too, were different – she wore a blue boiler suit, all frills discarded. Sometimes it frightened him to see how wholesale the effect of her education was on Rita. It was as if, while he watched her week after week, month after month, a new creature was emerging from the wreckage of the old: grub to chrysalis to butterfly, he thought, calling up an old analogy. Well, she hadn't quite reached butterfly status yet, but there was no doubt that the chrysalis-case was beginning to crack.

Rita clambered up into the train. Frank handed her the case. The door slammed. She pushed her head out, looking down at him. Frantically she said, 'I'll write to you. Every day. I've got your address in France.' They looked at each other; everything had already been said. 'Have a good holiday,' she added after a while. 'And don't go drinkin' too much, will you?'

Down the platform, a whistle blew.

'And don't you go staying up till all hours at campus parties and the like,' Frank warned her.

She grinned. 'I should be so lucky.'

'I mean it.'

'Oh, do you?' For a moment, both of them wondered just why he was being so vehement.

'Yes,' said Frank.

'All right.' She laughed. 'I promise I'll go to bed at ten o'clock every night with a cup of cocoa. And *Howard's*

71

End . . . That's if Howard shows up!'

They laughed; and at the same moment, the engine gave a shudder and, motors hammering, began to move. As the train started its forward glide and Rita's head was pulled away from above him, she leaned out further. 'Frank!' she called. He began to hurry after her, trotting a little to keep up. 'It's a pity I don't have my diary,' she shouted, her voice altered by an exaggeratedly stagey accent. 'One should always have something sensational to read on the train!' For a moment longer she watched him as his figure, laughing again, receded. Then she flopped back into her seat.

'Oscar Wilde,' she explained to her astonished fellow-passengers – which did nothing to diminish their stone faced mystification. As they glanced nervously at each other, Rita, giving them up for the bad job they were, settled down with a book. One thing about Summer School, she thought with sudden exhilaration, it won't be full of people who've never heard of Oscar Wilde.

At first, however, it was her worst expectations that seemed about to be fulfilled. She felt lost, excluded from the chatter all about, intimidated by the university atmosphere and by what seemed to her the confidence and certainty of her fellow-students. Many of them had, apparently, been teachers, civil servants, managers, and administrators. Who was she, after all, to try and compete with them?

'At first it was like I thought it would be,' she wrote to Frank. 'I didn't know anyone, and I was simply going to go home . . .'

Lost, she drifted through the grounds and buildings. She wandered up and down the stacks of the library, browsing moodily on titles. How much there was she didn't know – hadn't even heard of, for Christ's sake! Idly, she took down a book, and began to flick over the pages. Poetry. It seemed very vigorous – and comprehensible.

Beside her, a voice said, 'Ah! Are you fond of Ferlinghetti?'

'Frank,' she wrote, 'it was right on the tip of my tongue to say, "Only when it's served with Parmesan cheese" – but, Frank, I didn't. I held it back.'

The man beside her was round faced and rather boyish, with fair hair beginning to recede from his forehead. She said, 'Actually, I'm not too familiar with the American poets.'

The man, smiling, introduced himself: he was a tutor on the course, and modern American literature was his subject. He began to talk about Ferlinghetti, Corso and other West Coast poets, about Roethke and Berryman and Lowell. 'Frank,' she wrote, 'he started to tell me all about American poetry – and he wasn't even one of my official tutors! Oh, you'd have been very proud of me today.'

In far-off France, sunlit among the abbeys and chateaux, Frank read her letter and smiled. He and Julia were sharing a holiday with Brian and Elaine – pompous Brian, silent Elaine. Already, he was bored, with Brian's omniscience and the awe with which Julia received it, with Elaine's blankness, with his own lack of interest: even his own boredom bored him. He hankered after Rita's liveliness, and the purpose that his sessions with her had given his teaching life. No, he thought, that's an evasion: to his life, simply – all of it. 'A style of architecture unique in Paris,' blathered Brian, and 'Do you think so?' Elaine mooed, her voice empty of interest. Dropping back, Frank took Rita's letter out of his pocket again and began to re-read it . . .

Meanwhile, Rita was leaping her hurdles with grace and vigour. The next appeared in front of her on her second day. With two or three hundred other students, she sat among the clear, modern lines of the main lecture theatre and heard a wise, professorial talk on Chekhov. Leaning forward, Rita feasted. The professor, white hair flowing from a noble forehead and with a chin like the prow of a Viking ship, spoke reverently of the Russian master – his tightrope walk between comedy and tragedy, his genius for rendering boredom and despair dramatic, his instinctive awareness of the currents of love, hatred, ambition and frustration that flowed to the slow pulse-beat of country-house

73

existence. But at the end, Rita felt that something had been missed out. Chekhov had, hadn't he, a political relevance, especially in the light of the Revolution that would so swiftly sweep away the entire class from which his characters sprang? Why hadn't that been touched on?

Questions were asked for. As always, the audience sat as though spellbound – or paralysed. That evening, Rita would be able to write, 'Frank, there must have been hundreds of us in this lecture hall. But when the professor finished his lecture and asked if any one had any questions, *I* stood up. Honest to God – I stood up. Everyone was looking at me; I don't know what possessed me! I was going to sit down again – but all these hundreds of people had seen me stand up. So I did it! I asked a question!'

If the reality was a little more diffident than this suggested, it was not to be wondered at. Rita, on her feet, looked left and right as though expecting an attack. As the room quietened around her, her mouth dried. She cleared her throat; panic-stricken, she fumbled for words: 'Er . . . I was . . . I thought . . . That is . . .' She took a deep breath, looked down at the waiting professor, and finally plunged in. 'I was wonderin' if . . . er . . . if you think that Chekhov was showin' us the aristocracy as a decayin' class?'

The professor smiled. Rita, relaxing now in her seat, smiled back. 'This view of a Chekhovian aristocracy in decay – it is, I presume, one you have picked up from Dr Palmer's book on Chekhov? Now, whilst I myself . . .'

Rita, taken aback by this imputation of wide reading, abruptly called out, 'No!' Every pair of eyes in the hall focused on her. She flushed, but stuck to her guns. 'I mean, excuse me . . . but, no.'

'I beg your pardon?' The professor was frowning now.

'I didn't get it from that book. I haven't read it.' The silence around her suddenly seemed to her, not a menace, but an invitation. She began to speak, ready now to inform the whole world of her views on Chekhov. He must have had a political attitude of some kind, she said: there'd been unrest throughout the nineteenth century. Everyone knew that more trouble was brewing. Everyone could see that the point of conflict lay on the big estates. Chekhov must have had that background in mind when he wrote. He might not have been entirely conscious of it, but it must have affected the way he saw, the way he wrote . . . 'Frank, you couldn't keep me down after that. I've been asking questions the whole week. Mostly about Chekhov, because you know how familiar I am with Chekhov now.'

It was with relief that Frank came back to England. He'd had enough of being patronised by Brian, slighted by Julia, and ignored by Elaine. He was tired of the rambling monuments left behind by privilege, tired of the bland, dark-green beauties of the Loire Valley landscapes – too rich, he thought, like an over-furnished room. He felt a need for Rita's acerbic breeziness, for her irreverence, for her passion to learn and change and advance. He was humming quietly to himself, therefore, as he strolled once more across the familiar university lawns, still for the moment empty of students. This, he thought to himself, this is where I belong.

As he reached his usual entrance, he met the Bursar coming out. A short, straight-backed man with a bald head, the Bursar had habitually the expression of a person who has just been forced to eat something both outrageously exotic and predictably disgusting. Never was this expression more pronounced than when he happened to meet Dr Bryant. It was not unexpected, therefore, that now he should try to walk away without a word.

'Hullo, Bursar,' Frank called out cheerfully.

The Bursar stopped, disgruntlement in every inch of his spare frame. Frank, beaming, approached him. 'How are you? Another new term beckons, Bursar!'

'Dr Bryant!' The Bursar made the name sound like an accusation. 'You're back before term begins.'

'Preparations, Bursar – preparations!' He smiled sweetly, then turned away. 'Well, I can't stand here idling with you. There's work to be done!' He walked briskly towards the waiting doorway. Behind him the Bursar, speechless, watched him until he had vanished from sight.

In his study, Frank worked through some of his lecture

notes, outlined possible revisions to his course on the Romantic poets, and studied the new university directives that were beginning to accumulate as the next term approached. Then, glancing at his watch, he pushed his paperwork aside and hurried from the room.

He reached the station earlier than was sensible. With time to kill, he wandered slowly to and fro. At the bookstall he noticed a display: *Rubyfruit Jungle*, by Rita Mae Brown. He smiled to himself. It was time that he read Ms Brown – he still had, after all, the paperback Rita had lent him on the first day they'd met.

The clock hands jumped. Under the high roof, announcements boomed and cannonaded. Pigeons flew low over the heads of harassed travellers. The automatic notice board whirled and rattled like a toy. Frank read its ephemeral messages, and found the one addressed to him. *Platform 8*, it said, and he followed its directions. Glancing up at the station clock, he saw that he'd wasted too much time. If he didn't hurry, he'd be late. He hurried.

From the gate of Platform 8, passengers were already fanning out, spreading like an army bent on conquest. Frank, his head turning from side to side, began to scan them, first in expectation, then in slowly gathering dismay.

Quite close to him, Rita called his name. Puzzled, he swung round. 'Here! Frank! Over here!' And there, sure enough, she was – Rita returned, but once again transformed. She was wearing tight white trousers, a plain white shirt, and a loose blue jacket. A long white scarf was draped around her neck and shoulders.

'Rita! My God! What is this vision that I see before me?'

She laughed, pirouetted. 'D'you like it?' She struck exaggerated poses, like a model. 'I've got a completely new wardrobe. D'you like it? . . . Do you?'

Rita, he thought, has reached the inner suburbs. She's switched backgrounds. Is this where she'll stop? He picked up her bags. 'Well, it's certainly very . . . But did you actually manage to get any work done?'

'Work?' she cried. 'We never stopped. Lashin' us with it, they were. Another essay! Lash! . . . Do it again! Smack! . . .

Another lecture! Lash! . . . It was fantastic. I could've stayed for ever.'

They walked out across the forecourt to where Frank's car was parked. He stowed her baggage in the boot, then reached in and brought into the light a duty-free pack of two hundred cigarettes. He held it out to her. Smiling, she shook her head.

'Frank, I've packed up.'

He raised his eyebrows. Once she'd thought that cowardly. 'Congratulations,' he said, and threw the pack into the boot again. He opened the door for Rita, then walked round and climbed into the driver's seat. Rita was fumbling in her handbag.

'I brought a present back for you, Frank. It's . . . you know . . . not much. But I thought . . .' She held out a small, oblong box. When he opened it he saw, nestling inside, a rather smart, black ball-point pen. She pointed at it: 'See what it says. It's engraved.'

Frank held it up and studied it. In a neutral voice he read out the inscription. 'Must be used only for poetry. By strictest order. Rita.'

'I thought it'd be a gentle hint,' she said, a trace of uncertainty in her voice.

Frank began to laugh. 'Gentle!' he said. Carefully he replaced the pen in its box. But his thanks, she thought, watching him, were a bit subdued.

They drove out of the station and towards the outskirts of the town. Rita, puzzled, wondered where he was taking her, but he only smiled. 'You'll see.' Low hills rose on either side. Woods bunched, dark green, across gentle slopes. A river glittered behind bushes, as though signalling some bright but secret message. Frank stopped the car. From the back seat he took a box of sandwiches, a Thermos flask, and a couple of beer cans. 'Picnic,' he said. 'To welcome you back.'

Munching sandwiches, Rita sat contentedly against a tree-trunk. She watched the slow movement of the river down in the shallow valley. A heron flapped on slow wings above a pale green row of willows. 'What are we gonna be doin' this term, Frank?' she asked. She stretched, settling her head back against the tree. 'Let's do a good dead poet. One of the greats.'

Frank smiled at her phrase. Hadn't he once said something similar? 'I've got you just the man,' he said. He got to his feet and began to climb the slope to where his car stood parked at the roadside.

'Who?' she called after him.

'Aha! . . . I've been saving him for you.' He took a book from the glove compartment, and slammed the car door shut. 'They overcomplicate him, Rita,' he said, hurrying back down to her. 'Always they overcomplicate him.'

'But who is it?' She was laughing, intrigued.

'You won't overcomplicate him, though. You'll love the man.' He came to a halt beside her, one hand on the trunk against which she leaned. 'I was going to introduce him to you before – but I've been saving him, Rita.' He looked down at her for a moment, then opened the book and began to riffle through the pages.

'Who?' she asked. 'Who is it?'

Frank handed her the open book. 'Look . . . read this. Just read it.' She took the book and he leaned his back against the trunk, looking out across the wide valley. For a moment she read silently, then glanced up at him. She seemed to hesitate; then she began to read aloud.

Oh rose, thou art sick!
The invisible worm,
That flies in the night . . .

Her head had lifted; she was not reading any more, but reciting from memory.

In the howling storm,
Has found out thy bed
Of crimson joy . . .

Frank, turning his head to watch her read, realised with a sudden shock that she was speaking unprompted lines she knew by heart. He stared down at her, his expression dismayed and troubled.

And his dark secret love
Does thy life destroy.

Beaming proudly she looked up at him.

'You know it?' he asked.

Rita laughed like someone who's played a successful trick. And so, in a way, she had. 'Yeah,' she said. 'We did him at Summer School.'

Frank felt desolate – it was as if he'd been robbed of some precious heirloom. He'd hoarded this gift, looking forward to the time when he might give it to her. Now it had become valueless. He'd had visions of himself leading her when the time was ripe through all the cunning innocence of Blake – Blake above all, he'd been certain, would prove her poet. Now he'd been forestalled: Blake had been 'done at Summer School'. It was unfair! He felt battered by jealousy, almost physically assaulted. And he felt a kind of grief, so deep and pervasive it took his breath away.

'Blake at Summer School!' he said. 'You weren't supposed to do Blake at Summer School.'

Rita laughed happily. Delighted at his astonishment, she remained unaware of his dismay. 'I know. But we had this lecturer, and he was a real Blake freak.'

Frank nodded, taking the book from her. He flicked through the pages. 'So you . . . er . . . you've already done Blake? . . . You've covered all the *Songs of Innocence and Experience*?'

Rita laughed again. To him, it sounded more like jeering. 'Of course. You don't do Blake without doin' *Innocence and Experience*, do you?'

His heart sank further. It seemed to him from her tone that not only had they 'done Blake', but that they'd done him badly. For Rita, Blake was just another poet, a landmark among a hundred others on the literary landscape, little more than one more milestone along the marathon route of her course. He shut the book, holding out his hand. 'Come on,' he said, and pulled her to her feet.

Starting the car he asked, for form's sake, 'Where to?' As Rita hesitated, he added, 'Your mother's?'

But she had another surprise for him. 'Frank, would you drop me in town? I've gotta look at a flat. I've answered an advert.'

'To share?'

'Yeah.'

'Who with?'

'I don't know.'

The answer discontented him. She was beginning to complicate her life. She'd worked at Blake without a word to him, quite suddenly, when she'd not been ready. She'd simply followed where someone else had led, some tutor who didn't know her and had no concern for her progress. Now she was proposing to live with strangers, entering a situation that, by its nature open-ended, might lead anywhere. She ought, he felt, to keep her life under more control; she always had in the past, after all. 'Well,' he said grudgingly, 'you should be careful, flat-sharing. You don't know who you might end up with.'

She laughed, though not without astonishment. 'Frank! You sound just like me father!'

He grinned at her, a little self-consciously, but drove on without speaking. In town, Rita took a piece of paper from her handbag and gave him directions. They stopped in a street of tall Victorian houses, one of those well-proportioned terraces that had risen as testaments to a spreading late nineteenth-century wealth. Now, divided into flats, they held the transient, the determinedly unmarried, the elderly, the newly independent young, the bohemian and the trendy.

As he unloaded her cases, Frank asked, 'Are you sure you don't want me to come with you? It looks a bit . . .'

'What?'

'A bit seedy, as a matter of fact.'

She looked at him appraisingly, as though trying to determine what was the matter with him. Then, with a slight effort, she shoved her threatening irritation aside.

'Frank! If I end up as a white slave, I'll send you a postcard.'
She began to climb the steps of the house. 'Go on!' she
called back over her shoulder. 'I'll see you at the tutorial.'

He hesitated a moment longer, then with a slight shrug
climbed back into the car. Driving off, he felt disgruntled:
the day hadn't gone in the way that he'd intended. He'd
hoped to welcome back the Rita who'd gone away. Instead,
something had happened to her. She'd changed – and not,
he felt, for the better. The old rapport between them
had been disrupted, perhaps broken up beyond repair.
Rapport between teacher and student was a delicate thing.
Damage it, and it might wither. She shouldn't have read
Blake without him. Nor have decided to move without
asking his advice. He knew some perfectly reasonable
people from whom she might have rented a room. Instead,
she'd rushed off into an area of which she knew nothing,
and which looked distinctly raffish. What would happen to
her there? Probably too much – her work would be
interrupted.

And who, he wondered, savagely grinding gears, might
she meet?

*   *   *   *

Rita, left behind, watched his car out of sight. She'd sensed
something of his discontent, but couldn't see how it had to
do with, or really concerned, her. As she turned to the front
door with its array of scribbled names and shaky bell-
pushes, she became conscious of the sound of music.
Somebody was playing something rather grand extremely
loud. Strings moaned in emotional unison, the sound deep
and demanding. She searched among the names, found the
one she wanted, and pushed the bell. Nothing happened.
Only the music, she thought, began to swell out even more
loudly than before. She rang again, then hammered with
the knocker. Still no one came to the door. With a wry
grimace of resignation mixed with annoyance, she picked
up her bags and started down the steps.

Behind her, the door opened. Music poured out into the

street like the sudden flood when a dam bursts. A long-limbed, very slim young woman with black hair stood leaning in the doorway. Her clothes were loose, colourful – outrageous. Rita noticed a headband on which gold stripes glittered, an oriental waistcoat that matched it, and loose harem trousers that might have graced the concubine of a Caliph. And indeed the girl who stood there, with her big, black eyes and her fine, aquiline nose, her pale olive skin and air of arrogant eccentricity, might well have been the queen of some great potentate's seraglio.

'Er . . .' Rita muttered, a little taken aback. She cleared her throat. 'I come about the advert. You know – for sharin' the flat.'

The young woman smiled vaguely, half-closing her eyes. 'Wouldn't you just *die* without Mahler?' she said. She remained like that for what seemed to Rita quite a long time. Finally, seeing the slight smile on Rita's face, she pulled herself together and stood a little straighter. 'Oh, what *am* I doing? Come in! Come in!'

Rita heaved her cases through the door. The other, picking one of them up, led her across a nondescript hall, somewhat in need of minor repairs and major repainting, and into her apartment. Rita had an impression of space, of furniture islanded between stretches of bare floor, of a bright scattering of rugs, of the cascading green of plants drinking in the light from wide windows. Powerful, and clearly expensive, hi-fi equipment dominated the room. The music that came bellowing out of its speakers seemed to Rita so forceful and overwhelming, she was afraid that at any moment it would knock her to the ground.

'Oh, do say you'll take it!' the young woman yelled at her. Her dark eyes flashed. 'You're the first human being who's applied.'

Rita laughed. Try and get rid of me, she thought. This woman was the true, exotic, marvellous thing she'd been seeking. Everything was right about her – clothes, accent, manners, mannerisms. She was, clearly, a free spirit: a creature out of legend. 'Yeah,' she said. 'Yeah, I'll take it.'

'What?'

Raising her voice, Rita tried again. 'I said,' she shouted, 'that I'll take the . . .'

'What am I *doing*? This is madness!' The young woman turned down the stereo and into the sudden near-silence, murmured, sighing, 'But don't you just *adore* Mahler? Don't you love him?'

'Only on alternate Fridays,' said Rita.

The other burst out laughing, the sound of it clear and unaffected. She added a little scream of pleasure. 'Oh, darling, how *lovely*! But here, I promise you, you shall get to love him *every* day of the week. Come on – let me show you your room.' She turned up the sound again, asking as she did so, 'What's your name?' But Rita, yelling, knew that her reply hadn't been heard. Perhaps she'll never know it, she thought; perhaps we'll live here for years and never learn each other's names.

'Oh, Mahler,' cried the other. 'Wouldn't you just *die* without him?'

So began a new phase in Rita's life. Her new flatmate, it turned out, was named Trish. She was vague about her origins, apparently unconcerned over her future. She supported her exotic lifestyle by whatever means happened to offer – usually, by working as a waitress in some overpriced strip-pine-and-candles wine-bar, though she had been an advertising agency's receptionist, a manicurist, an art-gallery attendant, a film extra, and a researcher for a TV programme. Before that, apparently, she had been a student, though in what discipline never became apparent, nor whether she'd ever graduated in it. For Rita, the point was that she'd never met anyone remotely like Trish in her entire life. Or perhaps the real point was that, in her wilder dreams, she'd always hoped to meet someone like that. It was no wonder that Trish's ways, Trish's preferences and mannerisms, Trish's very character, instantly conquered and occupied her own.

Thus, a few days later, though not on time, there was a transformed Rita with her head round Dr Bryant's door. It was an altered head, too, with hair now allowed to flow loose and with no colour added to disguise its natural dark chestnut.

'Hello, Frank.' Rita's voice had taken on what it could of Trish's upper-middle accents, modified by her habitual trills and swoops.

Without looking up from the essay he was reading, Frank said, 'Hello . . . Rita, you're late.'

Rita came slowly into the room. She wore a red head-band and black jeans. A necklace of strange, knobbly stones hung around her neck. 'I know, Frank,' she said, in the same strained accent. 'I'm terribly sorry . . . Frank, wouldn't you just *die* without Mahler?'

At last Frank looked up, taking in her new outfit. 'Frankly, no. And what's wrong with your voice?'

'Nothing is wrong with it, Frank,' Rita replied, with what irritation her new accent allowed. 'I have merely decided to talk properly. As Trish says, there is not a lot of point in discussing beautiful literature in an ugly voice.'

'You haven't got an ugly voice. At least, you didn't have. Talk properly.'

'I am talking properly,' she insisted. 'I have to practice constantly, in everyday situations.'

Frank was aghast. What the *hell* was happening? In a frosty voice he said, 'Do you mean you're going to speak like that for the rest of this tutorial?'

Rita was lofty. 'Trish says that, no matter how difficult I may find it, I must persevere.'

'Well, will you kindly tell Trish that I'm not giving a tutorial to a robot!'

'I am not a robot,' Rita said like a robot. 'A robot I am not. I am not a robot. A robot I . . .'

'Rita! Stop it!' There was more appeal than command in Frank's voice. Rita, however, was stubborn.

'But, Frank, I have to persevere, in order that I shall . . .'

'Rita! Just be yourself!'

She looked at him without speaking, then gave a little shrug and, in her own accent, though sullenly, said, 'I *am* being meself.'

Frank raised his eyebrows, but made no reply. He walked over to the bookcase, and began searching for a book. His finger bumped over fat spines, gathering dust. In a low voice that did not disguise his irritation, he asked, 'And who the hell is Trish, anyway?'

'Trish? Me new flatmate.'

Frank came back to his desk, carrying the book. He smiled towards Rita, hoping for a more amicable mood, but she was looking out of the window. 'Is she a good flatmate?' he asked.

Rita whirled around, her face ablaze with her new enthusiasm. 'Frank, she's fantastic! She's dead classy. She's got taste – you know, like you. Everythin' in the flat's dead unpretentious. You know – just books and plants everywhere . . . I'm havin' the time of my life, you know, Frank. I feel young!'

He grinned at her as though he didn't know what she meant. 'Twenty-six is hardly old, Rita.'

She bounced up and down in the effort to make him see. 'I know, I know – but I mean I . . . I *feel* young. I can *be* young . . .' She turned back to the window and pointed towards the students she'd been watching on the lawns below. 'You know – like them down there.'

Frank had wandered back to the bookshelves. Now, with a little grunt, he pulled out the volume he'd been searching for. He flicked it open, smiling and nodding to himself. He walked back to the desk again. 'I'd like you to do an essay on Blake for me.' He smiled again, this time at her look of surprise, perhaps even protest. 'Yes, I know you're an expert on Blake now, but nevertheless I've not had the benefit of your wisdom on the subject.' He opened the book, searching for the passage he wanted.

Rita, her back to him, had strolled across the room. Glancing up at the bookshelves, she saw the gap left by the book he'd taken down. In the cavity gleamed the rich tints of a bottle of whisky.

Frank said, 'Now, I thought if we could look at this . . .'

'Are you still on this stuff?' Rita asked, her disapproving voice cutting off his words as though with a knife. Frank, looking up, followed her pointing finger. The bottle seemed to lurk in its own shadows: the skeleton in the cupboard, he thought.

'Still on it?' he said. 'Did I ever say I wasn't?'

'No. But . . .' She stopped, looking across the room at him in genuine bewilderment. 'Why do you do it, Frank, when you've got so much going for you?'

With a touch of bitterness, Frank replied, 'It is indeed because I have so much going for me that I do it. Life is such a rich and frantic whirl that I need the drink to help me step delicately through it.'

The irony was defensive and Rita ignored it. 'It'll kill you, Frank,' she said, simply.

He looked at her as though trying to calculate how genuine she was. Does she care, he wondered; how much does she care? He didn't ask, 'In what way does she care?' It was a question he didn't dare put, precisely because he knew that the answer would disappoint him. But then, after all, in what way did he care for her? 'Rita,' he said, chidingly. 'I thought you weren't interested in reforming me.'

'I'm not. It's just . . .' She stopped, almost as though embarrassed. Frank couldn't be sure, because embarrassment wasn't one of Rita's usual reactions. But in a moment she plunged on. 'It's just that I thought you'd started reforming yourself.'

'Under your influence?' He might have been laughing at her. He wasn't sure himself whether he was or not. He had been drinking less – until a week ago. What had happened a week ago? Rita had come back from Summer School, changed. 'Your influence?' he asked again, and watched her shrug. 'Yes . . . But, Rita, if I take the oath, if I repent and reform – what do I do when your influence is no longer here? What do I do when, in appalling sobriety, I watch you walk away and disappear – your influence gone for ever?'

'Who says I'm gonna disappear?' Rita demanded. But there was a chilly desperation in her tones.

'Oh, you will, Rita, you will.' Frank, needing her more than she needed him (tutors came by the dozen; there was only one Rita), knew by that very fact that she was bound to leave him and move on.

Rita, less involved, could allow herself to be stubborn.

'Why've I got to disappear? This course could go on for years . . . And when I've got through this one, I might even get into the proper university here.'

'And we'll all live happily ever after?' For a moment they looked at each other: they knew the kind of stories that ended like *that*. Then Frank gave a little snort, almost of contempt. 'Rita, your going is as inevitable as . . . as . . .' He groped for something suitably light.

'*Macbeth*?' she suggested.

Frank leaned back, laughing. 'As inevitable as tragedy – yes. But it won't be a tragedy, because I'll be glad to see you go.'

'Oh! Thank you very much!' But then, suddenly uncertain, she added, 'Will you really?'

'Be glad to see you go? Well . . . Certainly I don't want to see you stay in a room like this for the rest of your life.' He waved a hand at the book in front of him. 'Now . . .'

'You can be a real misery sometimes, can't you? I was dead happy when I came in here. Now I feel like I'm havin' a bad night at the morgue!'

Frank tapped the book, smiling at her in a way that was both friendly and neutral at the same time: a pleasant, teacher's smile. 'Well, here's something to cheer you up,' he said. 'Mr William Blake.' He held up the little volume like a flag of truce. In some way they'd got at cross purposes. It happened between them sometimes: some unspoken element crept in and distorted meanings, fuelled irritation, blunted understanding. Perhaps it was because, while she knew his role in her life, he couldn't really define her role in his. He wanted to change her, yet wanted her unchanged. He looked to her for honesty, yet helped her to overlay it with jargon and borrowed opinions. And then there was sex: he knew she was attractive, but refused to discover how far he was attracted. At the same time, he resented the fact that, as far as she was concerned, there seemed to be no sexual component in their relationship at all. She worried over him, as she might over an uncle. Or the family pet. He waggled the book again, smiling.

'Billy!' cried Rita, taking the book, accepting with it the

87

proferred truce. With neutrality re-established, they could pass on to neutral subjects. 'I wonder if he'd have become a famous poet if he'd been known as Billy Blake.' She giggled. 'Sounds more like the family butchers.'

Frank pointed out that he hadn't been a famous poet to himself. He'd written the poems that he'd been compelled to – by his emotions, his strange vision of the world, and by his sense of the divine expressed through the ordinary phenomena of life. It was that, he said, that he wanted Rita to think about – Blake's world, the way he saw the universe, the way he shaped it, described it, painted it . . . Cutting short his flow, she demanded references. What had other critics said? Where could she find the relevant passages? Feeling like Dr Frankenstein, Dr Bryant settled again to the nuts and bolts of his academic labours.

Rita, however, now had another mentor. Trish had opened to her an entirely new life, with an entirely new set of attitudes. It had never occurred to her that one's entire existence could be defined and lived out in terms of style alone. Trish seemed to float through life, as light as a balloon, as thistledown. There was no substance to her at all – just her voice, her clothes, her mannerisms, her wild hair, her dark eyes gleaming out of that long, patrician face. Music surrounded her as though to protect her from anything more substantial. She denied, it seemed, everyone's reality but her own. She drifted, self-created, through a self-created world.

It gave Rita a strange thrill of excitement and pride to be admitted into that world. She became, in effect, Trish's acolyte, an extension of her flatmate's character and activities. She changed her own style – in clothes, in hair, in conversation. In Trish's artificiality she found the reality she'd been seeking. She felt that she'd made it: she was an insider now. If Frank ever invited her again, she wouldn't prowl that pavement a second time, nor retire defeated.

She went to work with Trish in the evenings at the little bistro where her flatmate queened it, ostensibly as a waitress. Rita adored the place: students crowded it, there was talk everywhere, laughter, disputation. Smoke curled under the ceiling, posters on the wall announced long-dead exhibitions, forgotten plays, and defunct products. The tables stood close together, like wooden sheep huddling for protection. In headbands and pleated dresses from the twenties, Trish and Rita ministered to their raucous clientele, dispensing food which had long ago given up the attempt to live up to the excitements of the menu.

'Darling,' wailed Trish – it might have been any evening – 'could you take the order on Fourteen?'

Rita, who had obliged before, smiled acquiescence. 'Yeah, okay.'

'That horrible man keeps coming in to chat me up.'

Rita glanced across at the table. An innocuous-looking man was sitting harmlessly, apparently going through the menu item by item. Trish's world was populated by unsuitable swains, secret emissaries from her parents, agents of government, and potential rapists. Few people passed her scrutiny, swift though it usually was. Those who weren't dangerous were loutish, insensitive.

'He's not horrible,' Rita said.

'Darling, he's a *philistine*!'

Rita, her voice descending to a Groucho Marx rasp, said, 'Why bring his religion into it?' She smiled. 'All right – I'll get his order.'

'Oh, you're a love.' Trish looked thoughtfully at the salads Rita was balancing on her arms, preparatory to carrying them to the impatient hungry. 'Where are the real men these days?' she sighed. 'Why don't we get the likes of Shelley and Byron and Coleridge in here?'

Rita replied, coarsely, 'They'd smell a bit, wouldn't they?'

'Oh, you *are* a love,' Trish cried again, laughing. But in an instant she had sobered. 'Yes – yes, that's it. They're all dead, aren't they?' An expression of deep sadness passed across her face; Rita, still busy with her salads, missed it, and a moment later it had gone. 'Ah, well, never mind. At least one has one's vibrator!'

Laughing, Rita set off with her salads, spread them before those awaiting them, then crossed to Table Fourteen.

'Ready to order, sir?' she asked, her pad open.

Concentrating hard, the man began to mutter something about a mackerel paté. Writing it down automatically, Rita heard from behind her the high tones of animated debate.

'It wasn't! It wasn't, Tiger. Shaw wrote it in 1936.'

'No. It was *produced* then, but . . .'

The customer, clearing his throat, felt that perhaps he'd take the Persian Lentil Mornay. And, with it, a Catalan Salad.

'Shaw actually wrote *Saint Joan* ten years earlier: 1926.'

Rita snapped shut her little pad, and turned round. Flushed, the faces at the table behind her leaned towards one another; they shone with the excitement of dis-agreement. The boy who'd spoken last – Tiger, Rita had heard – was tall, fair-haired, with a broad, intelligent forehead and the glamour of good health and surplus energy about him. One of the others was pointing a pedagogic finger at him. 'Look, Tiger, I'm sorry, but . . .'

Rita leaned down towards them like some Homeric deity interfering in mortal battles. Her smile was serene, distant, minimal. 'Actually,' she said, 'Shaw wrote *Saint Joan* in 1924.' Silenced, the students gaped up at her. Still with the calm – and the generosity – of a goddess, she added, 'And would you like some more wine?'

In this somewhat high-handed way, Rita made new friends. To her, they seemed an extension of the world Trish had opened to her – her world now, she felt. Tiger and his circle took to her like a key-ring to a key. She was older than they, but not by enough to make her of a different generation. She knew the things they knew, and in many cases, such had been her frenzy to learn, she knew them better. But she also knew the things she'd always known, and which were strange to them: Rita had been street-wise when they'd still been shaking plastic rattles in their prams. For the first time, Rita found herself sur-rounded by the admiration of people whose judgment she respected. She began to think rather well of herself. In time, perhaps, she too might achieve the high style and easy command of a Trish.

Frank could feel his influence on her begin to wane. He'd been her Pole Star for so long, the one fixed point by which she'd steered, that at first he refused to believe that she was changing. When he realised that this was because he didn't want to believe it, he realised too that the change had actually occurred. He felt distraught, though he controlled the feeling. Her discovery of other relationships seemed, not a development in her, but rather a rejection of himself. He'd had her exclusive attention; having to share it with others, he felt diminished.

He stood at his window, looking down. Outside, a spring sun shone on the new, brilliant green of lawns and trees. For the first time that year, students lay sprawled on the grass, happy in a warmth that drew from their bones the memory of winter. Rita came strolling easily across the court. With a shock, Frank saw that she was now almost indistinguishable from the others. She wore faded jeans, a windcheater that proclaimed her support for – perhaps membership of – the New York Yankees. She carried the books under her arm with a casual air, like someone used to them. And of course, he thought, she *was* used to them now.

Someone waved and whistled: a tall young man, blond, with a wide, white grin. Rita waved back, then crossed over to him and his friends. Talk followed, accompanied by animated gestures; a book was produced. Rita, sitting down, flicked over some pages, pointed something out. The book was discarded: there was general conversation, sudden laughter.

By God, Frank thought to himself, she's made the transition! I've been the guide, and I've brought her through. But through to where, after all? Where was she now? Was this what she'd always wanted, or was it some other condition, some chimerical land with fool's gold for currency? Still, wherever it was, it was a long way from where she'd started. He sighed, and smiled wanly, before turning back to his own desk . . . But who the hell was the young man with the fair hair?

It was almost a quarter of an hour later that he heard her

feet padding up the stairs. She burst into the room, talking as she came. In a sudden time-warp, Frank remembered the first time he'd seen her. She'd come charging in then, too, loud, busy, terrified, domineering. He remembered bright hair, tight skirt, Rita Mae Brown and innocence. Now, here was this New York Yankee, skidding to a halt.

'Hi, Frank. Sorry I'm a bit late. I got talkin' to some of the students on the grass. I didn't realise the time.'

Frank allowed a little irony to relieve his feelings. 'Well, well – you talking to co-students, Rita!'

'Don't sound so surprised.' She almost bridled. 'I *can* talk now, you know, Frank.'

He made a wry little grimace; despite himself, nostalgia gnawed at him. 'And you used to be so wary of them, didn't you?'

'God knows why.' Thump went her books on the desk in front of her. 'For students, they don't half come out with some rubbish.'

'You're telling me?' Frank's comment sounded heartfelt.

'D'you know what one of them actually said? That as a novel he preferred *Lady Chatterley* to *Sons and Lovers*. I thought, I can ignore this . . . or I can put him straight. So – I put him straight.'

Frank licked lips that had gone suddenly dry. He noted with some surprise that he was nervous. Here he was, face to face with the new Rita, the Rita that he'd created – that Dr Frankenstein had created. And it is true that her certainties, her proclamation of cultural absolutes, seemed to him monstrous. But how could he persuade her that such wholesale acceptance of received opinion might be dangerous, and that no one could legislate for another's taste? 'I thought you said,' he murmured, 'that the student claimed only to prefer *Chatterley* as a novel.'

'He did.'

'So he wasn't actually suggesting it was superior?'

'Not at first. But then he did.' She chortled. 'He walked right into it!'

'So . . . you finished him off, did you, Rita?'

With a gesture of total disdain, she brushed the student aside as though he'd been a midge, or some nuisance equally ephemeral. 'Frank, he was askin' for it. He was an idiot. His argument just crumbled . . . It wasn't just me – everyone agreed with me.' She sensed his disapproval, without understanding how she'd aroused it. She thought that he shared her certainties: it was from him, she believed, that she'd learned to distinguish between the more and the less worthwhile. If she studied enough of the right opinions, she felt, all her opinions would be right. Then she and Frank would have identical reactions to everything, and these would be the correct reactions, rendered acceptable by the approval of the educated – people, that is to say, like Frank. It all fitted together, as exquisitely as marquetry. And if Frank really did dis-approve – well, there were others who thought better of her and her ideas. She said, 'Tiger was with us. Do you know Tiger? He's dead mad, you know.' She paused, looked swiftly at him, then away. 'I'd only known him for five minutes and he was invitin' me to go abroad with them all. They're all goin' to the South of France in the summer holidays . . . Slummin' it!'

Without hesitation, Frank snapped, 'You can't go!'

'What?'

Frank knew the look on her face, that look of the outraged child. He cleared his throat, a little uneasily. 'You can't go,' he said again. Her scheme was impossible – seemed impossible to him. Why? Why couldn't she go to France with Tiger? 'You've got exams,' he said, but knew it wasn't the real reason.

'My exams are before the holidays.'

'Well . . . You've got your results to wait for.'

They faced each other with a cold, weary hostility that was new. It's all finished, he thought, and felt a kind of panic grip him. It's all going wrong now. We don't under-stand each other any more. He needed her to be herself: as he watched, however, she was turning into someone else. At the beginning, they'd been warm together, intimate; he'd known her – hadn't he? – through and through. But it

93

was as if time were running backwards: the early closeness had faded and she was becoming a stranger. Only now, dealing with this person whom he no longer knew, did he begin to recognise how important her appearance in his life had been. She was only a student, he told himself, just another student – and that was true. But she'd been unique, quite special, and the way she'd been special and unique had been important to him. Now, he thought, she was becoming just like everyone else. If that was true, he'd lose her, whatever happened. Again that curious, cold panic gripped him.

'I couldn't go anyway,' Rita said at length. In his reverie, he'd almost forgotten what had started it. He looked up, saw that she'd crossed to the window and was looking out across the lawns, to the students sprawled in the sunshine. 'There's no way I could go.'

'Why?'

'It's all right for them. They *can* just jump into a bleedin' van and go away. But I can't.'

It's always the same yearning, he thought. The impossible desire to be something other than herself. The more she learned, the more masks she had to choose from, and the more elaborate they became. But, under those disguises, what would happen – what had already happened – to the real Rita? When she came across the practicalities of the world, as now, she could only see herself as defeated. Under all her hopes, her pretensions and ambitions, under all her bounce and hard work, Rita, he thought, placed a pretty low value on herself. With a sigh, he bent over her essay, beginning to skim through it again.

From the window, Rita said, 'His real name's Tyson. They call him Tiger.'

Startled, Frank looked up. Tiger would be the blond young man with the smile. Again the icy panic. She was sliding away, and his life would lose its only meaning. He jabbed at her essay with his finger. 'Is there any point my going on with this?'

'What?'

'Is there any point in working towards an examination, if

you're going to fall in love and set off for the South of . . .'

'What?' Her shocked tones sliced across his, silencing him. But he knew he'd gone too far. His own sudden bitterness surprised him. 'Fall in love?' cried Rita, outrage growing. He wondered how genuine it was, wondered whether she even knew. 'Fall in love with who? My God, Frank, I've just been talkin' to some students on the lawn. I've heard of match-makin', but this is ridiculous!'

'All right!' He wanted the conversation to end, wanted their ordinary relationship to be re-established. 'But just stop burbling on about Mr Tyson.'

'I haven't been burblin' on.'

He turned back to her essay, but found it difficult to concentrate. What the hell had they been talking about – really talking about, under the words, under the displays of temper, surprise, understanding, authority? It was all like some weird, reverse courtship; they were disengaging, getting *not* to know each other.

'Well?' she asked, sharply. 'What's me essay like?'

'Ah . . .' He drew a deep breath, and held the paper up, tapping the pile of other essays with his left hand. 'It . . . er . . . it wouldn't look out of place with these.'

His ambiguities were lost on her. 'Honest?' she asked, delighted.

'Dead honest,' he replied. After all, that was what she'd wanted. He was a good teacher, right? A marvellous teacher. If she didn't know what she'd lost, if she didn't care that she'd lost it, why should it matter to him? She'd pass her exams, and that was the main thing. He wanted to shout at her, 'You'll pass your bloody exams,' but what would have been the point?

He began to go through her essay paragraph by paragraph, just as a good tutor should.

It was laughter that a few days later gave Rita the first indication of how much Frank had returned to his reliance on the bottle. She didn't know that that was what it was when she heard it, though it puzzled her. She was out in the sunshine, but hurrying – Frank was giving a lecture, one of the open, big-event lectures of the term, a memorial to some long-dead academic, and she wanted to hear it. Or, rather, wanted to see him give it, to feel proud of him and pleased that he was her tutor. She'd imagined herself saying to someone, a neighbour in the audience, 'Oh, yes, know him well – been my tutor for ages.' But now there was this sound of laughter, baying out from the hall.

The hall itself was very grand, very high, with pillars, arches, heavy draperies and a great deal of marble. At one end there was a carpeted dais, about two feet high, and on it stood a lectern in varnished wood. In the body of the hall there was quite a press of students and faculty, as well as a number of outsiders: the occasion carried some prestige and, in any case, for the faculty and their friends a buffet had been provided. As so often, the lecture had become the price of a free meal.

The students were boisterous and noisy, because the lecturer was late. 'Why are we waiting?' they sang, sounding in their unmusical chanting somewhat like a football crowd. They slow-handclapped, they jeered, they suggested unsuitable candidates for the vacancy on the dais. Then the door at the side of the dais opened abruptly. The hall became silent. No one entered for what seemed a very long time – there was just an open door and several hundred pairs of eyes fruitlessly focused on it. Then Frank appeared.

He stood unsteadily in the doorway, looking around as though a good deal puzzled by what he saw. Then a wide, ineffable smile spread across his face, he made a little gesture, a half-wave of greeting, and lurched towards the lectern. That was when the laughter began. Clearly glad of the support, he leaned on the lectern, nodding all around as though greeting an assembly of acquaintances. The grin spread once more across his features and the laughter grew louder.

It was at this point that Rita, neat in a white jacket, came into the hall. She could see Frank draped over the lectern, being jeered by the students; to her he looked like someone who'd been condemned to the stocks. At any moment, she thought, the rotten fruit would fly. Her legs began to shake

96

and a kind of nausea overcame her. She sat down in a nearby seat and waited, not for disaster, which was already well under way, but for its outcome.

Frank raised a hand in unsteady command and, slowly, a near-silence settled over the hall. In a loud voice only a little slurred, Frank uttered one word: 'Poetry!' For a while it seemed as though this was all he intended to say. Blearily, he looked around the hall, giving little nods as though asking, 'There – what do you make of *that*?' But eventually, he continued.

'Literature,' he declaimed. 'What does it benefit a man . . . if he should gain . . . gain the whole of literature . . . and lose his own soul?' Frank stared about him belligerently, as though expecting an argument. But apart from the low hum of student comment, no one seemed disposed to say much. Clearly feeling that he'd made his point, Frank nodded again, then gave them all another of his wide, meaningless smiles. 'Assonance!' he announced. His arm swung round in a wide gesture, a movement of uncoordinated grandeur. 'Assonance,' he repeated, 'means getting the rhyme wrong!' He began to laugh to himself, like a man enjoying a private joke.

The Bursar, bald and bitter, got to his feet, the first in a whole file of the disapproving. Frank watched the exodus, still now and then chuckling to himself. He came out from behind the lectern. 'Terrible, isn't it?' he said. 'Yes, terrible – to take the name of literature in vain.' He began to laugh again, as he walked unsteadily to the edge of the dais and looked down at the expectant students. 'Like pissing on Wordsworth's tomb!' he cried, and fell off the platform.

The embarrassment thus removed, an enjoyable chaos took over. Some of the students near the front rushed forward to help. They lifted Frank, now totally disorientated and almost unconscious, and carried him out through the door beside the dais. From the rest of the audience there rose a scandalized babble. People had, they told others, expected something like this. Everyone knew about Dr Bryant, after all. There'd been that time when . . .

Swapping Frank Bryant stories, they slowly shuffled from the hall. On the whole, they felt their time hadn't been wasted: they'd been entertained, without the labour of taking in a long lecture. And they'd been present at an occasion that would be long discussed. They would be authorities whenever it came to be mentioned.

Rita sat alone, unmoving. She felt as if she'd witnessed the death of a close relative. Frank had destroyed himself, not just for her, but in front of hundreds of people. What the hell was the matter with him? Didn't he have everything she'd always coveted? And what did he do? He spat on it, spat on his students, on what they were learning, and on all the work he himself had done over the years. He made it clear that he despised everything that he'd spent all his life working for, working with. But where was the source of that terrible, corrosive contempt? And where the source of his self-destructive urge? 'The invisible worm,' she murmured: 'Oh rose, thou art sick!' She wondered if he'd passed what ailed him on to her, if he'd slipped into his teaching the same virus that had so completely undermined him. She'd have to see. She sighed and got to her feet. The great hall was empty. It looked pointless, overblown, like an empty theatre. Slowly she walked towards the door. All that learning, she thought, all that wisdom, the Georgian house, the lectureship with tenure, respect, affection – all that, and what had it got him?

By the following day, the wide nets of authority were closing in on Frank. The invitation was polite, but firm: would Dr Bryant please present himself, in the place specified and at the time decreed . . . Wearing gowns and serious expressions, they were waiting for him: the Vice-Chancellor and three senior professors, one a lady of censorious aspect, all gowned and preternaturally solemn. Ranged behind a table, they asked him to stand; he felt like the accused at a court martial. His behaviour, they suggested, could be regarded as a disgrace. The reputation of the university had been tarnished – the occasion, after all, had been semi-public. The memory of the great man for whom the annual lecture had been intended as a monument had been slighted. He himself had been rendered ridiculous in the eyes of the students and, by extension, so had the entire faculty.

'Doctor Bryant,' the Vice-Chancellor said, in tones of vibrant solemnity, 'we feel that this sort of thing must never, never be allowed to happen again!'

Frank bowed his head, in the submissive gesture prescribed by the ethologists; he was not unhappy to be dismissed by this little bench of magistrates. Outside, he took a deep breath, and began slowly to walk down the stairs. He held himself consciously erect, his head high. It was a little late for pride, but one had to make a show. Anyway, sod them! 'Sod them!' he muttered to himself. He imagined shouting it: he could hear the echoes rolling off the dressed granite of the walls.

At the foot of the stairs, her arms wrapped round her knees, Rita sat hunched and waiting. Frank stopped: somehow, she was the last person he'd expected to see. She seemed very small and rather forlorn, sitting on the steps like someone displaced, a refugee. He began to descend the stairs again, still moving very slowly. Sod them, he thought, was too feeble, too genteel.

'No – fuck them!' His voice was clear and crisp; it carried. 'Eh, Rita? Fuck them!' He stopped again, two or three steps above where she sat, and looked down at her.

For a moment, she studied him. Then she asked, 'Will they sack you?'

'The sack! God, no!' He moved down another step and sat on the stairs beside her. 'That would involve making a decision. Pissed is all right. To get the sack, it'd have to be rape – on a grand scale. And not just the students either – that would only amount to a slight misdemeanour. No, for dismissal it'd have to be nothing less than buggering the Bursar.'

Rita laughed despite herself, but then became serious again. 'Frank,' she said, 'even if you don't think about yourself, what about your students?'

'Well? What about my students?' He hadn't expected censure from her.

'It's hardly fair on them if their lecturer's so pissed he's fallin' off the platform.'

'I might have fallen off, my dear – but I went down talking!'

Rita gave a tight little smile, then climbed to her feet. 'Look, Frank, I'll see you next week, eh?'

He, too, stood up. 'We've got a tutorial,' he pointed out.

'You can't be in any state for a tutorial.' She shook her head. 'We'll talk about me Blake essay next week, when . . .'

'No!' He had things to tell her that he felt couldn't wait. 'No, you must stay. I want to talk to you about this.' He pulled her essay from his pocket.

'Is there somethin' wrong with it?'

He looked a little wildly around the university building. Footsteps echoed and there was the erratic rolling of voices uttering indistinguishable words. At any moment, with his luck, the Vice-Chancellor and friends would come down the stairs.

'Coffee,' he said. 'Come on.'

The Refectory looked like a cellar salvaged from some doomed monastery. A low, vaulted ceiling leapfrogged its way over squat pillars. Worn wooden benches stood at plain wooden tables. Frank carried their coffees to a table in a corner. When they were both sitting down, he pulled her essay from his pocket again, and laid it in front of her.

'What exactly *is* this?' he asked.

Rita looked at it for a moment, then up at him. Her face was set in the lines of a familiar stubbornness. 'It's me essay, Frank,' she said.

'It's . . .' he paused. Now that he sat opposite her, things that he'd wanted to say suddenly seemed less cut and dried than he'd believed. He *knew* what was wrong with her work, but found it hard to give that knowledge definition. 'Look,' he said. He tapped the paper. 'This passage about the poem *Blossom* – you've approached it as though the poem were about sexuality.'

'It is.' He saw from her face that she was adamant.

'Is it?'

'Well, it's certainly a richer poem if it's interpreted in that way.'

100

He hesitated, then sighed. 'Rita, we discussed it. The poem is a simple, uncomplicated piece . . .'

'Yeah? That's what *you* say, Frank.'

There it was: the nub of disagreement. Yet he knew he was right; he could feel the poem under the touch of his perception as though he were touching fine silk with his fingertips. 'You don't agree?' He waited, but Rita seemed to hesitate. He said, 'You think it gains from being interpreted in this way – your way?'

Again she hesitated, but her face had not lost its defiant expression. 'Is me essay wrong, then, Frank?' she asked.

He wanted to say yes: it was wrong-headed, false to the poem, demeaning of Blake. Yet it would do very well, it had the right sophistication, the right references – its very complications would make it more acceptable to many of his colleagues. 'No,' he said, reluctantly. 'No, it's not wrong. But . . .' He almost groaned: it *was* wrong, yet not in the way she had meant. Finally he shrugged and said, 'I don't like it.'

Rita laughed, the sound hard and derisive. 'You're being subjective!'

'Yes.' He laughed too, a little sheepishly. 'Yes, I suppose I am.' Once, he was sure, Rita would have responded to the poem as it actually was, to its simplicity and purity. The new Rita searched through it with a cold eye, discovered symbols, unearthed psychological possibilities, saw it as one more item in that useful adjunct in the examination hall, English Literature. That was the dichotomy – between the pure subjectivity and the corrupt objectivity. How could he as a teacher keep the balance between them? Keep the poem alive when Literature buried it?

As though aware of his thoughts, Rita asked, after a pause, 'If that essay was in an exam, Frank, what sort of mark would it get?'

'Oh, a good one,' he answered, wearily.

'Well, what the hell are you sayin', then?'

He tried to gather his thoughts. Had he a chance of convincing her? 'What I'm saying is that it's quite . . . oh, up-to-the-minute, trendy stuff about Blake . . . but there's nothing of *you* in there.' He slapped at the essay as though to punish it for its deficiencies.

Icily she said, 'Or, maybe, Frank . . . maybe what you're saying is that there's nothing of *you* in there! None of your views.'

He smiled, a little ruefully. She had a point; in a sense she was right. The trouble was that her essay didn't reflect her views either. They repeated what was fashionable, flashy little intellectualisms that probably won loud applause from Trish and her friends. But how could he argue that? 'Maybe you're right, Rita. Maybe that is what I mean.'

'When I first came to you, Frank, you didn't give me any views. You let me find my own.' If only you'd found them, he thought; if only you hadn't picked up all this academic lecture-room garbage instead. But he said nothing. Rita went on, 'You told me not to have a view. You told me to be objective. To consult recognised authorities. Well, that's what I've done . . . and these are the conclusions I've reached.'

Frank tried one last time. 'Your views I still value, Rita. But these *aren't* your views.'

She brushed this aside. 'I can have a mind of my own, can't I?'

'Oh, I sincerely hope so, my dear,' he sighed.

Belligerently, she leaped on this. 'What's that supposed to mean?'

'It means . . .' But he'd said all he could, explained more than she was prepared to accept. He said, 'It means . . . be careful.'

She leaned over the table towards him, her face white and tense. Her heart was hammering in her chest: she knew the moment had come for her to assert herself. She was a big girl now. 'For Christ's sake, Frank,' she hissed at him, 'I'm a big girl now! I can look after meself! Just 'cos I'm learnin' – 'cos I can read what I want to read and understand without havin' to come running to you every five minutes – you tell me to be careful!'

'It's because I . . . because I care for you that I want you to care for yourself.'

'I care for you, Frank.' Her voice was very quiet, though he had the sensation she was shouting. 'But just don't keep treatin' me as though I'm the same as I was when I first came in here. I do know the difference between Shakespeare and Harold Robbins. But you're still treatin' me as though I'm hung up on *Rubyfruit Jungle*.'

He hadn't realised how much she now resented his role in her life. Was it the case, he wondered, that he really hadn't noticed how much she'd changed? It seemed to him that the reverse was true. Yet didn't he feel already the pain of their approaching separation? Didn't he regret that the days had gone when he'd been her only guide into a world of which she'd known nothing? Well, yes, yes – but that was precisely because he realised by how much she wasn't the Rita he'd first met. Yet if he was honest, he knew that often he tried to maintain their old roles, often he grudged her the independence she'd gained, often he was jealous when he found that others had taught her things instead of him.

She put her hand out, checked by his troubled face. 'You do understand, Frank, don't you?'

'Yes.' He did, he did. 'Entirely, my dear.' He gave a little laugh, dry and false, and added, 'Hey, I . . . er . . . I got round to reading it, you know – *Rubyfruit Jungle*. It's excellent.'

Rita began to laugh. 'Oh, Frank – go away! Of its type it's interesting, maybe. But it's hardly excellent.'

That evening seemed to mark for Rita a personal declaration of independence. She began to arrive for her tutorials later and later. Once she telephoned him to say she couldn't make it. Then she stayed away without even telephoning. For two days he fumed; he thought she might call in or telephone, explain why she hadn't come, arrange a new day, a new time. There was only silence. He felt deceived, rejected. She must surely have realised long ago how important their sessions had become for him. She must surely understand that her success was his, that if she drew knowledge from him, he drew life from her. She must have seen how much he fed on her vivacity, her eagerness, her energy . . . But, of course, she might never have noticed anything of the kind. She couldn't believe that the Rita she'd been in the early days might have had great value for someone like him. She despised the person she'd been, and jeered at the idea that any part of her had deserved respect. In any case, that Rita had been abolished, transformed; the new Rita had no need of him. Or thought she hadn't.

'She thinks she's made it,' he muttered to himself, cup of whisky in his hand. He drank, pouring more. 'She thinks she's there. The world she wanted – talk, people listening to her . . . But who's to get her through her exams?' He decided the time had come to go out into the city and search for her. 'Bring-'em-back-alive Bryant, that's me,' he said to the picture on the wall, and marched out into the streets.

It was an hour or two later that Rita, looking up from arranging the evening's salads, saw his face peering in at her through the window. She realised that, dreaming of other matters, she'd been ignoring his steady tapping on the glass. Nervously, she licked lips suddenly gone dry: a thousand teacher's furies and parental tantrums had left their residue of fear. And then, besides, this was Frank . . . She hurried to the door and let him in.

'Hello, Rita,' he said. His smile was formal and chilly.

'Er . . . hi, Frank.' She looked at him for a moment, then turned away and went behind the wooden-topped bar. It was as though she felt she needed the protection. 'Frank, I'm sorry I missed the tutorial. We've just been dead busy and . . .'

'When you didn't arrive for your tutorial,' he said, ignoring her protestations, 'I telephoned the shop.'

'Shop?' She was bemused. 'Which shop?'

'The hairdresser's shop. Where I thought you worked.'

'I haven't worked there for ages, Frank.'

'So it would seem.' He watched her as, avoiding his eyes, she began to shuffle radishes again and arrange lettuce leaves. 'You didn't tell me.'

She shrugged, not looking up. 'Didn't I? I thought I had.' As he remained silent, she took the risk of meeting his gaze. So, once more, they faced each other, enigmas, antagonists. 'Frank, what's wrong?'

'It struck me there was a time when you told me every-thing.'

Exasperated, she snapped, 'I thought I *had* told you!' What the hell's the matter with him now, she asked herself fiercely. He's getting worse than Denny. And he isn't even my husband.

Frank nodded to the bottles lined up behind Rita. 'Do you think I could have a drink? Please – seeing I'm here . . . Oh, not for free. I'll pay.'

He laid coins on the bar, while Rita whirled angrily to the whisky bottle, filled a glass and slammed it down on the wood in front of him. 'Who cares if I've left hairdressin' to work in a bistro?' she demanded.

'I care,' he said, the glass half raised, as though he was giving a toast. He raised the whisky to his lips and drank.

'But why care? Why do you care about details like that? It's just boring, insignificant detail.' He shrugged. She thought so; she thought her life valueless. He had a different view of her. And, knowing the details of her life, he'd felt that he'd become part of it. Not any longer, it seemed.

'That's why I couldn't stand bein' in a hairdresser's any longer,' she said, her voice still angry. 'Boring, irrelevant detail all the time – on and on . . . Well, I'm sorry, but I've had enough of that! I don't wanna talk about irrelevant rubbish any more.'

Loftily, Frank asked, 'And what do you talk about here in your bistro?' But he was hating the conversation now. These days, when they spoke to each other at all, it was to be at cross purposes, either deep in misunderstanding or in quarrels.

'We talk about what's important, Frank. And we leave the boring details for those who want them.'

'And is Mr Tyson one of your customers?' he asked, savagely. Wrong, he thought; mistake. Did he care? He hadn't married the bloody girl, after all. And why give her so much of an advantage?

'Look, for your information, I do find Tiger fascinatin'.' Abruptly he felt sick, as after a blow. Unaware, she went

105

on, 'Like I find a lot of the people I mix with fascinatin'. They're young, and they're passionate about things that matter. They're not trapped – they're too young for that. And I like to be with them.'

Frank swallowed. He kept his expression calm. He said, 'So perhaps . . . perhaps you don't want to waste your time coming to tutorials any more.'

Yes, she thought. Right! She was free now, released into a wider world. What she felt for Frank was gratitude, not expectation: what he'd done for her belonged to the past. But these reactions panicked her. She said, 'Look, Frank, we were just too busy here. I haven't stopped coming altogether.'

'All right, then – come this evening.'

'Frank, I can't! I'm meetin' Trish soon. We've got tickets for *The Seagull*.'

He gave a thin, furious smile. 'Yes, well . . . when Chekhov calls . . .' But he knew he was being unfair. In the beginning, she'd never heard of Chekhov; now she was booking seats for his plays. Hadn't that, in some way, been the point? His recognition of this increased his anger and his despair.

Rita, with an exclamation of disgust, had turned away. To her back, he said, 'You can hardly bear to spend a moment with me now, can you?' Even to himself he sounded pathetic, ridiculous: a discarded lover.

Not turning round, Rita replied, 'That isn't true. It's just that tonight I've got to go to the theatre.'

'And last time you didn't turn up at all. Not even a phone call to say you'd had to cancel.'

'It's just that . . . there's so many things happening now. It's harder.'

'As I said, Rita, if you want to stop coming . . .'

'For God's sake!' She whirled round to face him, as desperate as he. 'I don't wanna stop comin'! What about me exam?' This was the chain that bound her, the condition of her last imprisonment: her Finals.

'Oh, I wouldn't worry about that . . . You'd sail through it, anyway. You really don't have to put in the odd appearance out of sentimentality. I'd rather you spared me that.' His bitterness did nothing to decrease the pain. He lifted his whisky and drank.

Rita pointed to the glass. Her finger was shaking. 'If you could stop pouring that junk down your throat, in the hope that it'll make you feel like a poet, you might be able to talk about things that matter, instead of where I do or don't work . . . And then it might actually be worth turning up!'

Frank put his glass down with exaggerated care. He smiled at her. 'And are you capable of recognising what does and does not matter, Rita?'

Harshly, she said, 'I understand literary criticism, Frank – and when I'm with you, that's what we're supposed to be dealing with.'

A long pause followed this. Then Frank nodded his head, like someone who is receiving instructions. 'Ah,' he said. 'You want literary criticism.' He fumbled with his briefcase, pulled out a sheaf of papers, and threw them on the bar. 'Literary criticism . . . Give me an essay on that lot by next week.' He jammed the briefcase under his arm, turning for the door. 'No subjectivity. No sentimentality. Just pure criticism.' He pulled open the door. 'An assessment of a lesser-known English poet.' He stepped out into the street. 'Me!' Quietly, he closed the door.

*   *   *   *

Later, he could never remember – had it been the evening of that day, or of another? The next, perhaps, or even the day after that? He remembered his coming home, but couldn't recall exactly when that had been. How long had he been drinking? He had no idea. He knew that he was drunk, but then it seemed to him that he'd been drunk for a long time. Now and then he would float up towards sobriety, but soon another alcoholic wave would carry him down, nearer to drowning.

Certainly he came home. He remembered the unsteady lock of the door, his slow fumbling as he tried to match its movements to those of the key. Standing in the hall, trying to get his bearings and his balance, he heard movement, some sudden manoeuvre in the living room. As he focused bleary eyes, he saw Julia standing in the doorway. She looked rosy; perhaps even flushed.

'Frank!' In her voice was greeting, warning, censure – a sense of confusion. Duly confused, he stared at her.

Muffled, Brian's voice came from the dining-room: 'Yes, Morgan – yes. But it's the publishers I'm worried about . . .'

'Brian was just passing, Frank. Called in . . . to make a phone call.'

Frank stared at her, wordlessly. His expression was blank; within, however, a great dawn had broken. He stopped himself from saying, 'Aha!'

'Yes,' came Brian's voice. 'You know why, Morgan . . .'

Julia looked Frank slowly up and down. Every line of her face now expressed a weary, familiar contempt. Poor Julia, he thought. Swaying slightly, he stood where he was: he seemed incapable of speech. Perhaps things had finally gone beyond words.

'I'll get you some coffee,' she said, and turned towards the kitchen. Left alone, Frank listened to Brian's determined negotiations. He giggled and, as though this had released him, began to weave his way towards the dining-room.

'Morgan,' Brian was saying, 'the advance they're offering is, as usual, an insult.'

Frank appeared in the doorway beside him, his face once more without expression. Brian raised a hand in greeting. Frank shook his head. 'Brian . . .' he said.

Into the telephone, Brian pointed out with some firmness, 'After all, I'm an academic author of some repute, and . . .'

By this time, Frank was tapping him on the shoulder and talking through his conversation. Not listening, Brian didn't hear him say, 'I haven't paid the bill.' He was sufficiently disturbed, however, to say, 'Hold on a second, Morgan. Frank's trying to tell me something.' He covered the speaker with his hand and looked inquiringly at Frank.

'Brian, the Telecom people disconnected us this morning.'

Gaping at him, Brian stood as though moulded in concrete. His skin had turned grey; only his knuckles shone as he gripped the receiver frenziedly. Frank leaned down and gently took it from him. He listened for a moment to its silence – the silence of death, he thought: the appropriate accompaniment. Into the instrument he said, 'Morgan – fuck off!'

Julia, as pale as Brian, came out of the kitchen doorway carrying Frank's coffee. Her dark eyes seemed enormous in her white face. She said, 'Frank . . .' then stopped. She could think of nothing to say to him. Perhaps she'd long ago said everything there was.

'Yes, oh faithful one?' Frank raised his eyebrows in an expression of ironic inquiry.

Brian, suddenly released from immobility, took a step forward. 'For God's sake! How could anyone be faithful to you, Frank? Julia's tried. She has at least tried. And what has she had in return? What have any of us had from you, Frank?'

Frank smiled, a bleak little grimace still smeared over by the softness of drunkenness. In the doorway, Julia was weeping, her whole body shaking as she tried to control her sobs. Frank said, 'Only my soul, Brian. Which I must confess is truly very little.'

Julia announced, unsteadily but with determination, 'Frank . . . I'm leaving you. Brian and I . . . That is, Brian's leaving Elaine. We're . . . we're going.'

It's like this, Frank thought. No great thunder of walls crashing. Just a small voice pronouncing sentence, the victim unconcerned, drunk, the real murderer feeble, apologetic, mouthing rubbish into a dead telephone. But that's what it was like – the world's end. Götterdämmerung. Eliot had been right: not a bang but a whimper. He reached out towards Brian and, seizing his hand, began vigorously to wave it up and down. 'Congratulations!' he said. 'Congratulations!' Dropping Brian's hand at last, he turned to Julia. 'I'm sorry, Julia. Better luck next time, eh?'

He walked out of the room, across the hall, out of the house. Stumbling along unfamiliar pavements, he knew it wasn't dismay at Julia's departure that was gnawing at him. She'd never been that important in his life. When he'd first seen her, she'd intrigued him. He'd wanted to have her, naked, in his bed: it had been lust, stirred largely by her aloofness. They'd got on well, for a while, but whatever had at one time approximated to love between them had long worn off. Their living together had become a continuing dishonesty, brought about more by inertia than anything else. If she and Brian could manage something better and truer, he wished her nothing but good fortune. Brian, too, come to that. He was an empty man, but, unlike Frank, with him it didn't matter. 'I'm empty because I know I'm empty – my knowledge of my emptiness drains me, day and night.' Thus Frank made his bitter comparisons. 'But Brian is empty and doesn't know it – he fills his emptiness with self-delusion.' And that would probably be enough for Julia, just as it had always been enough for Brian. Frank had a vision of the two of them, chattering happily into an unconnected telephone. That, it seemed to him, summed them up.

Then why was he experiencing this desolation? With bowed shoulders, he crossed unmemorable roads, ignoring traffic, weaving around anonymous passers-by. Perhaps he'd spend the rest of his life like this, walking to and fro in an undifferentiated, alcoholic limbo. At least with Julia he'd lived as though still connected with the world. However threadbare their relationship, it had at least existed. Perhaps he was now in essence dead. He'd lived as though alive, with someone to answer to, someone to quarrel with or to defy, someone against whom he could define his existence. Now there was no one – and at the precise moment when Rita, too, was sliding out of his reach: Rita, who had for a little while given his teaching career some sort of meaning, who'd opened to him long-forgotten vistas of hope, energy, honesty and laughter. He felt as though, after a short respite in the long decline of his life, he'd been shoved over the cliff again, to fall now without hope of rescue until he hit the ground. His life was once more pointless, as it really had been all along. 'The end of comfort,' he muttered to himself. 'The end of lies . . . Christ, what a prospect!'

When he came back to the house, it was empty. He walked slowly from room to room. What the hell did he want with a place like this? He'd be better off somewhere else, in some little studio that was convenient, practical, cheap to run. He opened the cupboard in the sitting-room and took out a full bottle of whisky.

'Thank you, Julia,' he said. After all, she might have taken the booze when she left. Too much of a hurry, he supposed. She would have done if she'd thought of it. He opened the bottle, poured out a glass and settled down to drink . . .

Again time vanished. Hours passed, perhaps days. Had there been night? Frank couldn't remember – certainly he'd slept. Hadn't he? Yes. Or passed out, more correctly. Yes, he'd been unconscious for a while, and on and off, had drifted into his own darkness and out again on more than one occasion. Had those been nights for other people, too? He didn't know. Anyway, what did it matter? But the ringing seemed to make it matter, and the knocking. Ringing, he thought; knocking?

He struggled to his feet and wandered out of the room and across the hall. With some difficulty, he opened the front door. Rita stood outside, her attitude uncertain, yet expectant. Wordlessly, they stared at each other.

God, he's a mess, thought Rita. His shirt was dirty, his trousers stained and rumpled. Stubble darkened his cheeks. His eyes blinked in the daylight as though it was too strong for them. They were yellow blotched, red-rimmed, bloodshot. His lips were dry and chapped. He seemed unsteady on his feet.

He said, 'What the hell are you doing here?'

For a moment he hesitated, then stood aside. Rita walked into his house. After the disastrous end to his first invitation, he'd never given her another. It had become a tacitly accepted fact that their common ground lay in the

111

university; his home belonged in a different dimension. Now she was through his front door and examining with a curiosity she didn't disguise the surroundings in which he lived. She thought the house grand enough, but its decoration conventional and rather boring. That'll be Julia, she thought – Julia's taste. In this conviction, she was correct; she was wrong in thinking that if Frank had decorated it, the house would have been vivid and fashionable. It would have been a comfortable slum, as his room at the university was. And as the living room had now become.

Rita stood just inside the door, looking around at the chaos of glasses, dirty plates, pieces of paper and discarded jerseys that littered it. Frank, behind her, was surprised. He must have been more active for longer than he now remembered. Here and there an empty bottle glittered, a reminder of just how he'd come to lose his memory.

'Where've you been, Frank? I've called your room a few times, but . . .' Her voice faded. It was clear where he'd been. 'I went to see Julia. She's nice, isn't she?'

Frank said nothing and, turning round, Rita now examined him as closely as she had the room. 'Frank,' she asked, 'are you sober?'

'If you mean, am I still this side of reasonable comprehension, then – yes.'

She pulled papers out of her bag. Frank found them familiar. They were his, weren't they? But how had Rita got hold of them? Then, in a blurred way, he remembered – there'd been that bistro, Rita busy, he himself angry . . .

Rita was saying, 'Because I want you to hear this when you're sober.' She waved the papers at him, his poems, the collected works. 'These are brilliant! Frank, you've got to start writing again. This is brilliant! They're . . . they're witty. They're profound. And full of style . . .'

He nodded, smiling, to encourage her. 'Ah! Tell me again . . . and again.'

'They *are*, Frank! It isn't only me who thinks so. Me and

112

Trish sat up last night and read them. She agrees with me.'
The words came tumbling out, tripping over each other
as her new enthusiasm drove them. 'Why did you stop
writing? Why did you stop when you can produce work
like this? What was it Trish said? . . . That it's more
resonant than . . . than purely contemporary poetry. You
can see in it a direct line through to nineteenth-century
traditions of . . . of, like, wit. And classical allusion.'

'Ah. Yes. Er . . . that's marvellous, Rita.' But she
caught none of the irony that he'd intended. Her eyes
shining, she was flicking through the poems again, reading
a line here and there. Oh, but this has to be put a stop to,
he thought to himself. Maybe she can shovel shit all over
Blake or Wordsworth – it doesn't matter to them, they're
big enough to stand it. And, besides, they're dead. But
this stuff is mine and it doesn't deserve much, but it does
at least deserve honesty. He reached out and took the
poems from her. He said, 'How fortunate I didn't let you
see them earlier. Just think if I'd let you see this collection
when you first came to me.'

'I know. I know.' She laughed excitedly. 'I wouldn't
have understood it, Frank.'

'You'd have thrown it across the room and dismissed it
as a heap of shit, wouldn't you?'

'I know!' She laughed, admiring herself now, pitying
her former self. 'But I couldn't have understood it then,
Frank. I wouldn't have been able to recognise and understand the allusions.'

He shook his head. 'Oh, I've done a fine job on you,
haven't I?'

Still she was blind to his irony. Her eyes shining, she
said, 'It's true, Frank. I can see now.'

For a moment he said nothing. What could he say, after
all? But he snapped out a bitter little bark of a laugh. 'You
know, Rita, I think . . . yes, I think that, like you, I'll
change my name. From now on I'll insist on being known
as Mary. Mary Shelley . . . Do you understand *that*
allusion, Rita?'

Bewildered, she frowned at him. Was it possible that

she'd displeased him? Despite her praise for his work? What the hell was the matter with him? And all this talk of Mary . . . Mary who? 'What?' she demanded. 'What allusion?'

'Mary Shelley. She wrote a little Gothic number called *Frankenstein*.'

'So?'

He reached out and took his poems from her. He shook them in the air. In the stale air of the room they rustled faintly, like dead leaves in a small breeze. 'This . . . this clever, pyrotechnical pile of self-conscious allusions is worthless, talentless shit. And could be recognised as such by anyone with a shred of common sense. It's the sort of thing that gives publishing a bad name! . . . Wit? You'll find more wit in the telephone book – and probably more insight. Its one advantage over the telephone directory is that it's easier to rip!' With vicious energy, he tore the papers in two. 'It's pretentious, characterless and without style.' And he tore the poems again, then a third time. Paper dribbled from his hands like snow.

'It's not!' Rita cried. 'It's not!'

'Oh, I don't expect you to believe me.' There was an infinite weariness in Frank's voice now. 'You recognise the hallmark of Literature now, don't you?' He threw the remaining fragments of paper on the table beside him. Some, falling, were lifted on the air and drifted for a moment to and fro, fluttered as though reluctant to descend, then fell. 'Oh, why don't you just go away? I don't think I can bear it any longer.'

'Can't bear what, Frank?' she demanded, in a voice made brittle by fury. She had made him the gift of her admiration, and he'd jeered at her, torn her gift in pieces. She wanted to see him hurt, humbled, physically destroyed. Had she had a gun, she would have shot him. 'What can't you bear?'

'You, my dear,' he answered in a low voice. 'You.'

'I'll tell you what you can't bear, Mr Self-pitying Piss-artist!' Standing over him, she shouted into his face. Her eyes were hard with hatred. 'What you can't bear is that

114

I'm educated now. I've got what you have – and you don't like it! Because you'd rather see me as the peasant I once was. You're like the rest of them – you like to keep your natives thick, because that way they still look charming and delightful . . . I don't need you! I've got a room full of books. I know what clothes to wear, what wines to buy, what plays to see. I know what papers and what books to read. I can do without you!'

'Is that all you wanted?' Genuinely surprised to hear her set out her achievement in these terms, he stared at her. 'Have you come all this way for so very, very little?'

'Oh, it's little to you, isn't it? It's little to you . . . who squanders every opportunity and mocks it and takes it for granted!'

Again there was a pause, one of those terrible silences that seemed sometimes to imprison them, and in which they communicated with a rawness much deadlier than words. Then, softly, he asked, 'Found a culture, have you, Rita? Found a better song to sing? . . . No. You've found a different song, that's all – and on your lips it's shrill and hollow and tuneless . . .' He shook his head slowly. It had all been for nothing, and now it was lost. 'Oh, Rita, Rita . . .'

'Rita?' White faced, she mocked him. 'Rita? Nobody calls me Rita but you! I dropped that pretentious crap as soon as I saw it for what it was. You stupid . . . Nobody calls me Rita!'

She turned from him and marched to the door, out of the room and across the hall. Not moving, he yelled after her, 'And what is it now, then? Virginia? Or Charlotte, is it? Jane? Emily? . . .'

The front door crashed to as she slammed her way out of the house.

For Frank, the sound of that door signalled defeat, the onset of a terminal solitude. His life, he felt, was finished now. He'd been given a glimpse or two of other possibilities, perhaps even a chance or two, but he'd . . . what were Rita's words? He'd squandered every opportunity, he'd mocked it, he'd taken it for granted.

For Rita, the crash of the slammed door seemed more

like the sharp crack of a starter's pistol. Even as she regretted her quarrel with Frank, she experienced a feeling of release. She'd begun her new life – her *real* life. She owed a great deal to Frank, but in the end she'd outgrown him. He should have realised that, shouldn't have tried so desperately to hang on to the past. It was sad that they'd parted as they had, but he hadn't left her much alternative. He simply wouldn't accept that she had other influences in her life now – Tiger and his friends, and Trish. Above all, Trish.

In the months that she had lived with Trish, Rita's admiration for her flatmate hadn't diminished. Trish, floating above the mundane in a dimension of her own, Trish, with her exotic clothes, Trish with her mysterious background, her slow, amused drawl, her insouciant way with money, work and friends – Trish still epitomised for Rita the kind of personality that she most hoped to grow into. For, with all her carelessness and dreaminess, Trish became dramatically intense whenever the arts were under discussion. Her views were always so firmly given, her reactions so total. She seemed almost to swoon at certain passages of music, at certain poems, before certain pictures. To be sure, these varied from time to time, but, as she said herself, life would be so *boring* if she became predictable. One had, hadn't one, always to leave oneself open to the true reaction of the moment? The very volatility of Trish's opinions seemed to Rita not only fascinating, but a guarantee of their sincerity. Nor did it diminish the influence of these opinions in the least when Rita saw that they were couched in the fashionable terms of a Sunday-newspaper review. On the contrary, it seemed to show that Trish and the reviewers, using the same language, were on a level, sharing a certain authority. As Rita sometimes put it to herself, when she grew up – really grew up – she wanted to be just like Trish. Thus it was with no great sense of loss that Rita settled to a life without Frank. Sometimes, working at her books, she missed his guidance, missed even the reassurance of his voice, but moments like that were rare. Most of the time, she was happy: her life was filled with animated talk, with a good deal of posing, not always recognised, with busy nights at the bistro and late-night sessions listening to Trish's Mahler collection. Sometimes it bothered Rita that, when she herself flagged and had to go to bed, Trish would keep on, riveted by the music, sprawled on a couch or sitting cross-legged on the floor, listening through the small hours and on into the dawn. She wondered where her friend found her energy, wondered at the strange brilliance of her eyes, her sometimes feverish manner, her apparent dislike of darkness, silence, and solitude. But such doubts were transient, swallowed by admiration, shared jokes, affection, and the constant talk.

One warm day in early summer, Rita could be seen running down a street. Her denimed legs twinkled, her heels clacked on the pavement. She raced towards her own house, panting with effort, leaped up the stairs and in. From the front door of the flat, she called for Trish. Only silence answered her. Frantically, she looked for her coat: she'd need it later.

'Trish!' she called. 'It's time!'

She ran into the sitting-room. The coat lay across a chair and she reached for it. 'Trish,' she called again. 'Come on – we're gonna be late!' She threw the coat over her arm, turning for the door. 'You know we should be at the bistro by . . .'

She stopped. There was silence . . . And suddenly she became aware of the record, turning on and on silently, the needle softly clicking. But that wasn't it. That wasn't it. It was the flash of white that she could see behind the sofa, the gleam of skin: an arm stretched out, pale, gleaming in the reflected light of a late-afternoon sun.

'Trish?' she whispered. 'Trish?'

Slowly she approached. Trish lay behind the sofa. Her head was thrown back, the eyes, not quite closed, stared through their long lashes at the ceiling. Closer to, Rita could hear the rattling unease of her breathing. A line of thin spittle drooled from her open mouth.

'Oh, Christ!' Rita said. 'Trish!' For a second longer she

117

stared. Then she was running for the telephone.

The day splintered into episodes. The blue flashing light of the ambulance, flickering across the sunshine. The unexpected tenderness of the men as they laid Trish on a stretcher. The strange, trapped silence inside the ambulance as, sirens howling, it raced through crowded streets. The disciplined speed of the nurses in Casualty. Then the long vigil, the lonely wait without news, suspended between Trish's death and survival, as outside the summer darkness slowly enclosed the city.

In the empty flat, the telephone rang, then rang again. It had done so on other evenings. When answered, though, Frank had put his own receiver carefully back on its cradle. What did he want; after all; what could he say? 'I want you as you were, so that I can be as I was'? It wouldn't be true; it was, in any case, impossible. Yet he could ask Rita how she was getting on, offer to help her with any problems, suggest short cuts to examination success. He was still her tutor, wasn't he? He had a role in her life, officially endorsed. He tipped the glass he held, swallowing whisky. Certainly he had a role. More, he had a duty. He poured more whisky, gulped it down. 'See, the thing is, Rita,' he said to the empty room, 'I do have a duty.'

Out on the street, some unknown street, Frank couldn't remember having left his house. He grinned. It had been a miraculous transition. Blearily, he looked around, trying to work out where he was. There were low houses, terraces built for Victorian artisans, now garish with unlikely colours. Here and there a door sagged, a window gaped darkly, its glass lost. Then there were little craft shops, shops selling artists' materials, antiques, cut-price radio equipment, or gleaming handmade wooden beds. An Indian restaurant, an egg-and-chips caff, a take-away Chinese, a crowded bistro, a little kebab house . . .

On unsteady feet, Frank turned, walked back the way he'd come. A bistro! That was the place. Rita's Bistro. That's why she hadn't answered the phone. She worked in a bistro – this bistro. That's where he'd come before to meet her. What harm if he looked in now? He pushed into noise, smoke, laughter. Someone was shouting. Waitresses bustled between tables, long-haired, in jeans and tee-shirts, distinguishable from the customers only by the officious alertness of their manner. Everyone was young, assertive and loud. A barman with a heavy moustache stood where Rita had been when she and Frank had spoken there. Frank pushed his way towards him. As he went, he was forced from time to time to steady himself – here on the back of a chair, there on the shoulder of a seated student. The room, it seemed to him, had been set adrift on some over-turbulent ocean. Noticing him, a few of the students laughed; among them, those who had been Rita's friends. Tiger, as usual the centre of the group, didn't join in the laughter. He watched Frank with sober, even anxious eyes.

At the bar, Frank pointed with shaky finger at the whisky. About to speak, he found himself facing the all-denying headshake of the barman. The moustache moved. It said, 'You've had enough, mate. Sorry.'

'No,' Frank muttered, hazily. 'No . . .'

'Yes,' said the barman, firmly. 'Yes.' Slowly, but not without menace, he moved out from behind the bar. 'Come on! Out!'

'Rita . . .' Frank spoke petulantly, as though the other was hiding her deliberately. 'I want to talk to Rita.' He articulated the words with precarious precision.

'Never heard of her, mate.' The barman clamped a large hand on Frank's arm. 'Come on!'

Frank shook him off, in a sharp, irritated movement. It also unsteadied him: he staggered back a step or two before regaining his balance. The room continued to sway upon its invisible ocean. 'Rita,' he said again. 'She works here.'

'You've got the wrong place, mate. No one called Rita works here.' The barman grasped Frank's arm a second time, more firmly than before. He began to pull on it, trying to lead Frank towards the door. Bemused, Frank grabbed a pillar and resisted. His head, he felt, had become too large for his body. He allowed it to droop, still anchoring himself against the barman's pull.

'Now come on!' the barman said, savagely. He bent to give Frank's arm a heave, dragging him free of the pillar. 'On your way!'

Frank moved forward unsteadily, unwillingly. Why was Rita hiding? He held onto the back of a chair, looking with unfocused eyes about him. His feet began to slide from under him as the barman applied pressure.

'Hello, Dr Bryant. Anything wrong?' Frank stared at blond hair, blue-grey eyes, wide mouth, a concerned expression. Wasn't that a face he knew? It was a face Rita knew.

'He's pissed, that's all,' the barman explained.

'Mr Tyson,' Frank said. 'Where's Rita?' A look of uncertainty crossed Tiger's handsome face.

'Look, I've told you,' the barman told Frank, 'there's no one . . .'

'It's all right,' Tiger murmured. He nodded reassuringly, first at the barman, then at Frank. As the barman dropped his hand, Tiger took the arm very gently, almost tenderly. He began to move slowly towards the door, an anxious Frank shuffling along beside him. The barman watched them for a moment, then shrugged. If it wasn't the bloody students, it was their bloody professors! Christ, how he hated the university crowd! . . . Scowling, he went back behind the bar; one day, when he'd seen enough, he'd explode with the pressure of cynicism building up within him.

Still being moved gently towards the door, Frank asked, 'Have you seen Rita? She's . . . er . . . You know – she works here.'

Light dawned; Tiger's face cleared. 'Do you mean Susan?'

It was Frank's turn to look baffled. 'Oh . . . yes . . . Yes, I suppose I do.'

Tiger said, 'She's not been in tonight.'

Frank nodded, his look of anxiety deepening. He stopped, frowning. 'You see, I forgot to remind her . . . About her examination tomorrow.'

'Oh!' Tiger tried to urge Frank on again. 'She might be up at the Flamingo,' he suggested. 'There's a dance on there.'

Frank nodded like a man who understands everything. As gently as Tiger, he pulled himself free. 'Thank you very much, Mr Tyson,' he murmured. With a smile and a little wave, he turned for the door. Tiger watched him as he stumbled towards the street.

He called something after Frank, some warning, a piece of advice. Dr Bryant had surely had more than enough; he'd be better off at home, in bed. From the doorway, Frank waved again.

'If you see her,' he called, 'will you tell her? Nine o'clock.' Then he was out in the little street again, unbalanced by the clear night air. For a while he stood holding a wall, uncertain whether he'd be able to remain upright or not. The giddiness passed, however, and he began to walk down the pavement, trying to set his feet down before the ground had a chance to move too far.

He might have looked down shallow slopes, over dark roofs, past spires, and seen, as he walked laboriously on, the lights of the hospital where Rita sat and waited. Around her, other people sat, alone or in couples, bent over their private needs. They hugged their fears to them, staring at the floor or at each other as though expecting revelations. The silent waiting room offered them no comfort. Now and again a nurse would come and speak with one of them, or a name might be called, there'd be a sudden muted bustling; then the stillness would settle once more. For Rita, nothing of this really impinged on her thoughts. She sat in her own cocoon of shock, trying to make sense of what had happened.

Trish had tried to kill herself. The fact was clear and she understood it. Yet it was a fact she couldn't fit into the other reality of Trish herself. It couldn't be a fact that applied to the Trish she knew. Therefore, either it hadn't happened, or it had happened to some Trish she didn't know at all. Yet it had happened; here she was, at the hospital, waiting for Trish to recover or go into her final decline. So the Trish she knew hadn't ever really existed, or hadn't existed as she had seen her. Rita didn't know how to accommodate this realisation: Trish had become so important to her, had drawn from her so much admiration, that now to discover that all along she'd been an invention, part-truth, part-fiction, was more than she could face. It was a conclusion from which her mind slipped, like metal from glass. She simply couldn't accept it.

A soft tap on her arm snapped her into the present. A nurse was bending over her, whispering something: Trish was all right, was recovering, could be visited. She lay in the muted lights of a curtained cubicle. Somewhere out of sight, a man groaned to himself rhythmically, and a little further off a woman screamed for a nurse. Trish lay very still. Her skin seemed to shine; it was bloodless, with the unpleasant sheen of the sick. Her hair was bedraggled, sweat-tangled, spread over the little pillow in twisted rats-tails. The black arcs under eyes made her look as though she hadn't slept for many days, and Rita thought that perhaps she really hadn't. The eyes themselves, though, were steady enough, watching Rita as she approached. Sitting down on a chair that stood by the bed, Rita found herself beyond words. Nothing she could say was likely to avoid danger; in the end, she chose the riskiest question of all.

In a very quiet voice, she asked, simply, 'Why?'

Trish turned away her head. She looked at the wall, then at the ceiling, as though perhaps they might offer answers. Finally she said, in a tone of unutterable weariness, 'Darling, why not?' Without her expression changing in the slightest, tears started from her eyes and began to roll down her pale cheeks.

'Trish,' Rita said, leaning forward and putting one hand on the other's arm. 'Trish, don't. It's all right. Don't cry . . . You're still here.' Even as she said it, she cursed herself for an idiot.

'That's why I'm crying!' Trish attempted a thin, dry laugh. 'It didn't work.' Her voice rose. 'It didn't fucking work!'

'But Trish . . .' Still Rita couldn't bring herself to believe that the cool girl she'd known, with her records and her easy dismissal of life's tribulations, her dramatic presence and outrageous clothes, could really have wished for an ending to it all. 'Trish, you . . . you weren't *really* tryin' to kill yourself? You were just . . .'

'Just what, darling?' Again those dark eyes were on her, looking steadily and very deep. After a moment Trish laughed her desperate laugh again. 'Poor Susan. You think I have everything, don't you?'

'Trish, you have!'

'What?' Trish smiled, and, looking into Rita's eyes, held her. 'Music? Paintings? Literature? . . . Well, yes – when I look at a beautiful picture . . . or listen to poetry, to music . . . I can live then – live inside it. But, you see, darling . . . the music always ends. And then there's only . . . life, really.' She smiled once more, a thin-lipped twisting of her face that seemed more tragic than her weeping. 'And life itself never quite lives up to the promise of the music.'

Rita could offer no reply to this. She sat silently, still holding Trish's arm, feeling as though in some way she must have failed. She was Trish's flatmate after all; she should have been more aware of how Trish was feeling, more alert, readier to help. She bent her head, trying not to cry. When she raised it again, Trish had drifted off into a gentle doze.

For Frank, meanwhile, the world had become entirely music. It howled and bellowed around his head, it took his bones and rattled them, its deep rhythms seemed to vibrate in his very bowels. Lights flashed, glowed and faded, changed colour, then dimmed into a twilight shot through with lightning. In this hellish universe, demons of unlimited and inexhaustible energy leaped and stamped and twirled and shook. Unsteadily, he wandered through the intermittent brightness. A large man, of a threatening and unpleasant aspect, put a hand on his shoulder. Frank, nodding as amiably as he could, asked about Rita. The large man appeared to have no

123

information to offer him, nor any suggestions to make
except that Frank should go home, as quickly as he could.
Or, as the large man actually put it, 'Come on, grandad,
it's past your bedtime!'

It was a student once more who came to Frank's rescue.
Well, well, he thought, pleasantly astonished, here was
the self-righteous Lesley! But Lesley had left her inhi-
bitions and her sense of rectitude in the tutorial room.
Here, with skirts flying and bouncing breasts, she seemed
to gleam. With soprano yells of glee she dragged Frank
away to the dance floor. Later, he remembered turning
and stamping as he tried to hear the music, by that time
only a great roaring inside his skull. Someone, he thought,
passed him a joint and he drew on it, taking down the
acrid marijuana smoke and feeling the top of his head
begin slowly to lift. Then lights, smoke, music, dance, all
tumbled into a single confusion. All he was certain of was
that he hadn't found Rita.

For Rita, too, there now came new confusion. Half
asleep herself at Trish's bedside, she pulled herself
together as a nurse came into the cubicle. She bent over
Trish, shaking her gently. Trish opened her dark eyes. For
a moment she looked blank, then consciousness, and with
it anguish, took over her expression.

'Come on, love,' said the nurse, 'give us a smile. Your
mum and dad are here.'

And there they stood, an elderly couple, grey with
anxiety and fatigue, he in a battered cap, a brown, ribbed
cardigan and baggy olive-green trousers, she with a scarf
round her hair and a bright red coat worn at the elbows
and the cuffs. A triangle of lining hung below the hem.
Rita looked from them to Trish, then back. They seemed
to belong to Trish no more than had the suicide attempt.
Yet that had been real; so, too, were these parents – the
flesh-and-blood reality.

'Pat!' cried Trish's mother. 'Oh, Pat, we've been so
worried about you!' The accent might have been that of
Rita's mother; it was hard, clipped and working-class. It
carried no echo of Trish's languid tones. Perhaps when

Trish had been Pat, she'd spoken in the same way.

Rita moved away from the bed. Trish was weeping again, while her mother held her in her arms. The father looked embarrassed, uncertain: the emotion in the scene was too raw and he'd simply switched off. Rita knew him as she knew her own people – he was a carbon copy of the men she'd known all her life. She leaned against a doorpost. God, she was tired! She could do with a drink, something strong that would blaze in her chest for a moment and warm and revive her. Maybe that's why Frank drinks the stuff, she thought. But the mother was turning to her, smiling, saying she was glad that Pat had found a friend.

'Yeah,' Rita said, nodding, smiling back. 'Yeah, we're great friends . . .'

Frank, alone, stood at that moment swaying in the darkness that covered the university lawn, covered the university, the city, the entire hemisphere. Frank thought that perhaps he could feel the darkness, moving against him like water: it might be that it was keeping him up. It's all that *is* keeping me up, he thought, and began to giggle. He lifted his right hand in the air, found that it held a bottle and put it back down again. He lifted his left hand. He giggled once more. He yelled, 'Bursar!'

Waiting, Frank drank from the bottle. After a moment he shouted again. 'Wake up, Bursar!' He could hear his voice echoing off invisible walls. He began to laugh, great shouts of laughter that rolled across the night. 'Come on, man!' Lights began to go on, the little squares of brightness spreading at a speed Frank found very satisfactory. Above him, a new light joined the others; the Bursar's silhouetted head poked out into the night. Frank raised both hands, waggling the half full bottle at him: 'Bursar! Join me in a drink!'

Other heads were by now outlined against a wide array of windows. Students were watching, there were other members of the faculty, and probably a handful of visiting dignitaries. There usually were a few around, Frank remembered. Once more he laughed, the sound rather

125

exultant and definitely loud. He waved the bottle so vigorously that a few drops spilled out over his hand.

'Dr Bryant!' The Bursar's voice was harsh, hoarse with fury. It came from above like that of some vengeful angel. 'Dr Bryant – go to sleep!'

As Frank stared up at him, he withdrew his head and slammed shut the window. A moment later, his light had gone out.

'Right,' Frank called up. 'I shall. Goodnight, Bursar!' He turned, threw himself full length on the grass, then drew up his knees, cradled his head on his arm and closed his eyes. Had he really intended to go to sleep? Later, he was never quite sure. But as his eyes closed, he began to snore, overtaken by fatigue, alcohol and the reaction to excitement of a man of fifty.

He would awake with aching joints and stiffened muscles under a dawn sky that, grey still, showed every promise of turning to a cloudless blue. At about the time that, doubled up and with one hand massaging the small of his back, he was making his way towards the gate and a taxi home, Rita was walking slowly down the steps of the hospital. Trish's parents had gone, and Trish herself lay sleeping peacefully. The crisis was over.

She strolled unseeing through the empty streets. A few early workers cycled by; a boy in jeans and a red tee-shirt delivered newspapers; and a milkman rattled from house to house. Rita noticed none of them. Her own thoughts walled her in, keeping out the world. If Trish's crisis was over, hers was not. Trish's crisis had triggered profound reactions in her – Trish had been for months the central goddess in her pantheon, the one desirable model, the incarnation of all the goals she'd set herself. Now Trish had proclaimed that she was a flawed goddess, that the goals were inadequate, perhaps meretricious. She turned out, in fact, not to be a goddess at all – turned out, what's more, not even to be Trish.

For a moment, Rita was furious. She'd been deceived! Lies had been told her, and on their basis she'd rearranged her entire life. She'd been persuaded to build her new life

126

on lies. Bloody Trish, playing her games, then drawing other people into them . . . But that wouldn't do. She should have been able to see through Trish. If she hadn't, what use had been her years of effort, her education? She'd have seen through her once, all right. No Trish would have been able to dazzle her in the old days!

That meant, though, that she'd had qualities once which she'd lost since, or laid aside. She remembered Frank, and Frank's poems. She'd held the collection up and said, 'These are brilliant.' And what had Frank said? That he was lucky she hadn't read it when she first knew him: 'You'd have thrown it across the room and dismissed it as a heap of shit . . .' She'd thought that he wanted her to remain a barbarian, but all he'd wanted was that she should remain honest. He'd seen through Trish, even if all he'd had to go on was Trish's product: Rita herself. She'd been misled by appearances, by easy options, and by shallow attitudes. Life was more difficult than that, and so was learning. She'd become a phoney, a self deceiver, just like Trish. Someone negligible, laughable. She'd forgotten the distinction between real and false. She'd thought that, by covering herself with a few of the right trappings, by draping herself with a few of the right opinions, she could simply jettison her past, just drop it and forget it. But that set up contradictions in one's life which eventually created intolerable strains. Trish had nearly died of them.

She drifted into a tobacconist's, bought cigarettes, and wandered on again. Smoking, she walked slowly down unfamiliar streets, vaguely aware that all around her the morning traffic was building up. What was it Frank had said? 'Have you come all this way for so very, very little?' She'd turned on him, but perhaps she should have listened. Perhaps she should have given old Frank the benefit of the doubt . . . But then, look at him. Committing his own slow suicide, courtesy of the distillers. Of course, he'd tried, had his own great vision, then failed to make it real and watched it fade. Maybe alcohol revived it, or revived the feelings it had given him.

Briefly, it induced an artificial euphoria, a desperate forgetfulness; but that wasn't for her, either.

What she had to do was to recover her ear. She'd had it once – in the old days. It was like the ear of a good musician. When he heard a false note, he cringed. So had she, and jeered, too: she heard her own voice – 'Go away!' Christ, but her old self would have had some jagged things to say to the person she'd become!

A sudden blast of noise – a car horn, people shouting – made her look up. Familiar faces grinned at her out of the windows of a van. In the midst of them shone the bright hair and white smile of Tiger.

'Hey!' he yelled. 'Susan! Where you goin'?'

Where indeed, she asked herself. She said, 'For a walk.'

'Wanna lift? Come on.'

'No. It's all right. I wanna walk.'

Tiger nodded, accepting this. 'Where were you?' he asked. 'You missed a great party.' The others set up a supporting chorus of whoops and yells.

Rita smiled wanly. 'Yeah? . . . Well – see you.'

Tiger, with a little 'please yourself' grimace, pulled his head in through the window. The engine note strengthened, and the van moved forward. But a moment later, it had stopped again and Tiger's head reappeared. 'Hey!' he shouted. 'Saw your tutor.'

'What?'

'Your exam's this morning.'

'Oh!' But it sounded like information from another world.

'If I was you, I wouldn't sit it. Examinations merely reinforce the bourgeois ethic.'

Jesus, she thought. Is that the crap I've been listening to? The van started again. Tiger's voice came floating back to her: 'Don't forget you're comin' to France . . .'

The van clattered off, and, turning a corner, vanished. 'Bye, bye, Tiger' she thought to herself. She wandered on, her thoughts fragmented, disturbing. It was as if she was drowning – her whole life seemed to pass before her eyes. Conversations she'd long forgotten repeated themselves in her head, old faces floated up from the twilight of her memory, old lovers embraced her. She felt as if her life was a parcel which had burst: the contents were cascading all about her, out of control, in no sort of order. She was assailed by chaos.

She found herself back at the flat and for a while wandered through its silence, staring at Trish's plants and records as though in them she'd find answers to the questions that plagued her. In the end, the stillness drove her out: it had seemed the stillness of death. Without realising that it had been her destination, she found herself again in the streets where she'd grown up. The pavements were full now, of people with pinched faces hurrying to work, a few early shops were opening, and crowded buses whined along the roadways.

Someone called to her. 'Susan! . . . Susan!' Turning, she saw a once familiar loose smile, dark eyes, a mop of black hair.

'Hiya, Denny,' she said. Beside him stood a shy, pasty girl, with pale straight hair, pale face, and yellow dress. Pregnant, she bulged. Her smile signalled contentment.

'This is Barbara . . . Susan.' Denny introduced his present to his past. 'Oh,' he added quickly, 'you don't call yourself that any more, though, do you? It's Rita now, isn't it?'

Rita smiled at him. It wasn't worth getting into. She asked him how he was, then asked Barbara when her baby was due. Rituals, she thought: she felt a stranger.

'Oh, I've got another three months yet.'

'It's gonna be a boy, though, isn't it, eh?' Denny was forceful, jovial. Barbara looked up at him and they smiled at each other. He turned to Rita. His eyes seemed to say, 'See what you missed.' Aloud, he asked, 'I believe you're doin' very well at the college, aren't you?' Rita shrugged; she didn't think she was, as it happened. 'I hardly recognised you,' he said, laughing. 'You really look the part now.' He gave Barbara a nudge. 'Doesn't she, eh? Looks the real student – be on drugs and demonstrations next.'

They all laughed, friends together. Then Denny turned to Barbara, putting a protective arm around her shoulders. 'We gotta go – goin' up to the hospital for a check-up.' He smiled at Rita. 'I always go with her.'

'It's good to see you, Denny.' Rita smiled back at him. 'Look after yourself. And . . .' – she gestured at Barbara – 'look after them two.'

'Oh, he does, you know,' Barbara murmured. 'He's very good.'

'I know,' said Rita, and watched them walking, intertwined, up the now crowded pavement. It could have been me, she thought; knowing that it never could. She gave a little shiver. She'd escaped, but it had been close. Christ, she'd had to fight to get clear; she remembered the long, bitter battles with Denny and her father. And where had she escaped to? What had her victory brought her? Trish, drooling out her life behind a sofa. The contempt of her tutor. Friends pickled in clichés, vibrant with slogans. Easy options, fake ideas, shallow attitudes . . .

She flung up her wrist, and stared at her watch. Turning on her heel, she began to run.

Her breath was rasping in her throat, but she made it. She clattered up the university steps and into the great hall with seven minutes to spare. Still panting, she found her desk. Great portraits stared haughtily out above the rows of aspiring heads. Chandeliers hung from the distant ceiling. Intimidating walls frowned down as though to turn the great room into a prison. The invigilator stood up and began to speak – they would begin at nine a.m. precisely; they'd have three hours, during which they'd not talk to anyone; if they wanted more paper a raised hand would ensure that they'd be supplied. He looked at his watch. 'It is now . . . nine a.m.! You may turn over your papers and begin.' Nervously, the students set about their examinations.

The silence seemed almost palpable. It wrapped itself round her, stifling, enervating. Around her, heads bent over paper, hands traced endless skeins of words. Rita, her eyes blank, stared into a distance only she could see.

She thought of her hours up in Frank's study, thought of how patiently he had set before her the riches she'd sought. Poetry, prose, a banquet of literature, garnished with the means to appreciate all she sampled; she'd sat at the table, then thrust back her chair and marched away as though the meal had been finished. He'd tried to call her back, tried to explain that there was much more she had to taste, much more she had to learn. But she'd lost her appetite; turning her back, she'd left him at the table.

As she thought about her original ambitions, Frank's effort to help her fulfil them, and her own false conviction that they'd been attained, the minutes raced by. Still her question paper remained face down, unread. Her head lowered, she stared at its blank back, not noticing what she was looking at. It made a screen on which to play her memories. Abruptly, she focused on it. A clock had struck. Had a whole hour passed? She shook her head, swallowed, and came out of her daze. Turning the paper over, she frowned at the first question. Her eyes widened. Involuntarily, she laughed, the sound shocking in this dedicated silence. Around her, others looked their disapproval. Ignoring them, she picked up her pen and began to write.

Busy now, she didn't see a door in the side of the hall open a quiet inch or two. Eyes peered through, searching – Frank's eyes, searching for her. In a moment, they steadied. She had been seen. The eyes narrowed a little as Frank smiled to himself. The door closed.

Two hours later the university buzzed and bubbled with the collective relief of students who have sat an exam. Everywhere, excited voices exchanged experiences, answers, doubts, and convictions of success. Rita, energized too, raced through the crowd, making for the stairs. She hurried up them, two at a time, bursting through the still-sticking door into Frank's cluttered study. The room was empty. She looked around, disappointed, then quietly closed the door. She loved this room, loved its untidiness, its odd comfort, the way it was dominated by books. She loved its colours – the faded reds

131

and browns and blues of the volumes on the shelves, the dark leather of the armchair, and the golden wood of the desks. She loved the piles of paper on every available surface, the books in disordered piles, the yellowing ceiling. She stood once more before the picture: erotic, she'd called it on her first visit. Like Frank, she'd hardly looked at it after that. But, yes, she supposed it was erotic. She stared out of the window: the play of light and shade on the façades opposite, the contrast between granite and lawn, the meanderings of students and staff below – all made her happy, as though she was looking out on a kind of perfection. With a sigh, she turned away from it, making for the door again. Halfway she stopped, intending to scribble a note for Frank.

The door opened. Frank entered, backwards. When he turned, she could see that he was carrying two small packing-cases. He glanced at her, curiosity and satisfaction combined in his expression, but said nothing. He put down the cases, then crossed to the bookshelves and began to pull out books. With his arms full, he turned back to the little crates, to pack the books into them.

'Have they sacked you?' Rita asked.

'Not quite.' Not looking at her, he went on with his packing.

'Why're you doin' that, then? Packin' your books?'

He paused, and finally looked at her. His smile was a little sheepish. 'I . . . er . . . Well, last night I made rather a night of it. So they're giving me a holiday. Two years in Australia.'

She watched him as he went back to his packing. 'Did you bugger the Bursar?' she asked.

He laughed. 'Metaphorically,' he said. He frowned at the books arrayed in front of him, then took down three or four.

'What did Julia say?' she wanted to know.

'Bon voyage.' He held the books out to her and she began to pack them.

'She's not goin' with you?' He shrugged and shook his head. For a few moments they worked without speaking.

Then, in a hesitant voice, she asked, 'What you gonna do?'

He laughed again. 'What do you think I'll do? Australia's a paradise for the likes of me.' He stood still, examining her. With a little shrug, he said, 'For Christ's sake, why did you come back here?'

'To tell you you're a good teacher.' They faced each other, almost as though about to quarrel again. Then he snorted, made a gesture disclaiming compliments. She said, 'Thanks for entering me for the exam.'

'That's all right.' He turned away, picked out more books for packing. 'I know how much it had come to mean to you.'

She nodded, biting her lip. She said, 'You didn't want me to take it, did you?' She watched him as he made a non-commital gesture. Nothing had really been as certain as that. 'I nearly didn't,' she went on. 'I didn't start for ages. I sat there while everyone else was scribblin' away – just thinkin'. About what you said. About what you've done for me.'

Not turning round to her, he said, 'What I've done for you is . . .'

'Shut up!' If he spoke now, analysing, criticising, he'd spoil everything. 'I'm doin' the talkin'. That's what's wrong with you – you talk too much.'

He smiled; briefly, he'd recognised a Rita he'd once known. 'You think you did nothin' for me,' she said. 'You think I just ended up with a load of quotes and empty phrases. Well, all right – I did. But that wasn't your doing . . . I was too hungry for it, Frank. I didn't question anything. I wanted it too much – so I wouldn't let it be questioned.' Her smile now was a little tremulous. 'I told you I was stupid.'

Frank tried to interrupt. 'No, you're not . . .'

'Listen – if I say I'm stupid, then I'm stupid. Right? Now, don't argue!' He laughed, but she didn't join in. There was a pause, then she said in a low voice, 'It's like Trish . . . I thought she was so cool and together. I got home last night and she'd tried to top herself.' He whirled

133

round, startled. She raised a hand to stop him speaking. 'Magic, isn't it? She spends half her life eatin' health foods and whole-foods, and the other half tryin' to kill herself . . . I was thinkin' about it all. When I should've been doin' me exam.' Again she paused, but then lifted her head and managed a little laugh of her own. 'D'you know what the first question was, Frank? "Suggest ways in which one might deal with some of the staging difficulties in a production of Ibsen's *Peer Gynt*".'

'And you wrote, "Do it on the radio"?' He bent, placing books in the packing case.

'I could've done,' she said. 'And you'd have been dead proud of me if I'd done that and rushed back to tell you. Wouldn't you?' Her voice became more intense. 'But I chose not to. I had a choice. I did the exam . . . Because of what you'd given me, I had a choice. I wanted to come back and tell you that . . . That you're a good teacher.'

Silently, Frank worked his way down one more shelf, picking out books, piling them in one or other of the crates. He felt strangely calm, in some way completed by her return. He said, 'You know, I . . . er . . . I hear good things about Australia. Everything seems to be just beginning out there.' He turned, books in both hands, and looked squarely at her. 'The thing is – why don't you come as well?' He took a deep breath, like someone coming up from a long time under water. 'It'd be good for us to leave a country that's just finishing for one that's just beginning.'

For a moment she stared at him, trying to read his expression. What was he offering her? Marriage? Concubinage? Permanent studentship? Or nothing more than friendship, companionship? She lifted her gaze. In the gaps left by the packed books, empty whisky bottles stood in dusty rows. They looked like lines of meths drinkers, waiting in the shadows for some expected handout. She said, 'Frank, if you could get threepence back on each of those bottles, you could buy Australia.'

'You're being evasive,' he told her; but smiled.

Then you be more direct, she thought. Tell me what's

really on offer. Aloud she said, almost submissively, 'I know . . . Tiger's asked me to go down to France with his mob.'

'And will you?'

'I don't know . . .' She turned away, running her fingers along the edge of a packing-case. Australia flashed like a vision – white beaches, foam flowering on the surf, deserts, mountains, the curve of Sydney Bridge: travelogue material, deliberately misleading, designed to tempt. Against that, there stood Tiger, with his smile, his cool chat, his easy clichés: 'bourgeois ethic', she heard again. She shrugged. 'He's a bit of a wanker really. But I've never been abroad . . . And there's a job I've been offered in London.'

He waited, but she seemed indisposed to be more definite. 'What are you going to do?' he prompted.

'Dunno. I might go to France. Might go to London. Or carry on with me studies . . . I might even just stay here and have a baby.' She glanced sideways at him, as though she was slightly ashamed of this possibility. 'I don't know. But I'll make the decision. *I'll* choose . . . I dunno.' Her voice trailed off. She'd thought that she would be decisive. Now the moment had come, she found decision beyond her.

Frank nodded briskly. From the back of a shelf now half emptied of books he picked up a package. 'Whatever you do, you might as well take this with you.' He handed it to her, not meeting yer eyes.

'What?' She held the parcel in her hands, confused. Was Frank playing some sort of joke on her? She ripped away the paper. A delicate blue fabric was revealed.

Frank said, 'It's . . . er . . . well . . . It's a dress, really. For an educated friend of mine . . . I bought it some time ago.' He watched Rita shake out the dress and hold it up against her. 'I . . . er . . . I don't know if it fits. I was rather pissed when I bought it.'

Rita, looking down at herself, observed the daring of the dress's cut. 'An educated woman, Frank? And this – is this what you call a scholarly neckline?'

Frank laughed. 'When choosing it, I put rather more

emphasis on the word "woman" than on the word "educated".'

Rita studied him, still holding up the dress. Slowly she lowered it and, with great care, began to fold it again. 'All I've done is take from you,' she said. 'I've never given you anything.'

'That's not true!' Frank cried. But the things she'd given him were impossible to define. She'd saved his life, even if later she'd let him drift on towards oblivion. How could he explain all that to her? While he hesitated, she cut in decisively. 'It *is* true! I never thought there was anything I could give you.' There was a new gleam in her eye. 'But there is . . . Come here, Frank.'

He watched her, not moving, caution in every line of his body. 'What is it? What are you going to do?' He looked as though at any moment he might flee the room.

'Come here,' she said again. She pulled a chair out from under the desk beside her and tapped it with an imperious gesture. 'Sit down here.'

Frank, not moving, stared at her in bewildered alarm. She rubbed her hands together in what seemed to him an ominous manner.

'I said, *sit*, Frank!' Rita slapped the chair hard. The sound snapped across the room like an explosion. Frank, half intimidated, walked slowly to the chair, hesitated, then sat down. His eyes looked anxiously at her over his shoulder. Slowly she approached him, a strange expression of triumphant determination on her face. Her eyes were bright and she was still slowly rubbing her hands together. Suddenly she reached out, her hand whipping past Frank's body. Involuntarily, he cringed back. From a jar on his desk, where it stood among chewed pencils and exhausted ball-points, she took a large pair of scissors. She said, 'I'm gonna take ten years off you, Frank!'

With the competence of long practice, she began to cut his hair.

*　　　*　　　*　　　*

136

Rita craned her neck, trying to look through, over, then around the crowd. Her denim-suited body stretched as she stood on tiptoe, glaring towards the entrance. Where the hell was he? Just behind her rumbled the narrow conveyor belts which passed passengers' baggage through the X-rays of airport security. Through the glass wall of the corridor, she could see the concrete apron with its deployment of airliners, each with its tail in the air like an excited puppy. A stream of passengers moved constantly by her – tall fathers in checked caps, harassed mothers cuffing over-excited children; honeymooners already intertwined, hips and shoulders apparently glued together; commercial gentlemen blasé about their five hundredth trip, grandmothers terrified over their first. All hurried past her, laden with hand baggage, bright with the plastic bags of last-minute shopping, their eyes already on the departure lounge, the waiting plane, the distant destination. But where the hell was Frank?

In modulated tones the airport informed its passengers of an imminent departure. 'This is the final call,' it said, 'for Flight BA 297 to London Heathrow. Would all remaining passengers please go to Gate 7.' Rita's lips were dry. If Frank missed this flight, he'd miss the flight from London to Australia which it fed. Yet there was no sign of him. A cold, even light fell from the high windows on a world full of strangers. Where was he? What should she do if he didn't come? What could she do?

In the distance, a head bobbed among others. It bounced, it dodged to left and right, it approached at speed: Frank, arriving at last and, thank God, at least running.

'Frank!' shouted Rita. 'Frank!' As he came closer, she began her scolding, her voice audible among the subdued murmurings that filled the airport buildings. 'Where've you been? We're gonna be late! It's takin' off in a minute. Come on! . . . Come *on*!'

But Frank wasn't coming on. Instead, he had halted; with the flat of his hand he was gentling her as one might a horse. He said, 'Your results were posted at the university this morning. I've been to pick them up.' He handed her a long, brown envelope. 'Go on – open it. Open it!'

Rita shook her head. She clutched the envelope, but otherwise seemed not to realise that she had it. 'Frank . . . Oh, we haven't got time! Come on . . .'

'Open it,' Frank said, calmly. 'I want to know.'

Behind him a security guard called out a warning. The gate, he said, was about to be closed. 'If you don't come right away, sir, I'm, sorry, but you'll miss your flight.'

'Frank!' Rita screamed at him, but he remained unmoved.

'Go on!' he ordered, nodding at the envelope. With a little moan of despair she ripped it open.

'Right' she said. 'I've failed. Okay? Now will you get on that bloody plane!'

'Failed!' Frank's bellow seemed to scythe through the building, cutting off all other sound. He grabbed the paper from her, glanced at it for a moment, then looked up at her. 'A pass with distinction,' he said, slowly, 'is not a failure.'

He began to smile, a great grin that spread across his face like the warmth of a new day. She could feel herself respond, could sense the laugh rising within her. He looks very good in a suit, she thought; he looks terrific with his new haircut.

Frank suddenly stepped forward and folded her into a crushing embrace. She could feel his body against hers: she had never really thought of him as owning a body. He'd been a head, a mind, a mentor. Now his warmth pressed in on her, his strength was holding her. Did they kiss? Later, she thought they might have. But, if so, it was briefly, gently, a pressure that hinted at what could have been, at relationships unrealised, unrealisable. Then he was away, bag swinging, sprinting for the closing gate. She shouted after him, a touch of desperation in her cry. 'Frank! Frank!' He checked and looked back. Their eyes met for what, remembering it, she thought a disproportionately long time. She swallowed. 'Thanks,' she said.

He smiled, turned away, and ran towards Australia.

Rita stood where she was for a while, staring down the corridor after him. As she turned away, her foot kicked paper. Slowly she picked up the announcement of her success. She looked at it a moment, then neatly crumpled it in her hand and, as she, too, began to walk away, dropped it in her pocket.

Just once she hesitated, looking back as though expecting him to follow her, as though imagining that she might follow him. Then, her back firmly turned, she walked away towards the new life that awaited her.

As she walked, she could hear the gathering whine, the roar, the overwhelming scream of engines building to their fullest power.